Dedication

It is my HONOR to dedicate this **sequel** to **God Don't Give U Nothing U Can't Handle** to all who believed in Sharhonda Genise as an auther when I didn't even consider myself to be. I dedicate this to you. I hope it can live up to the bar I set with **God Don't Give U**, admitting that I didn't trust myself to be able to write ½ the story being told in those 207 pages in its sequel. I gave it my best shot!

Sometimes you have to get out of your own way to realize your worth and make way for the bigger picture. There was a life-changing opportunity that presented forcing me to make the change I knew I should've made because that would be better for me. I went out on a limb from my comfortable box and was able to seize that opportunity to do better and make the best out of it. This is one of the benefits. There is definitely more to come!

Best Regards,

Sharhonda Genise

For Eugene Bates
1940-1995

Introduction

No body would ever find out what really happened to him, I tried to convince myself. I mean, the man was a bully. He bullied the guys at work and the few people he called his friends were all scared of him. He tried to pull that mess at home but I wasn't scared of him. He was an old ass drunk who *used* to be a force to be reckoned with. That time was long gone. I told him a million times to stop fuckin' with me and did he listen? Hell no. I warned him every time he got up in my face that I would kill him and he thought it was all some big joke. Now look where we are. Here he is, all burned up and only about 3 feet under and I'm standing out here in the goddamn rain waiting for Lamille's ass to hurry up and get over here.

"Damn, girl, I told you to BE here when it got dark. I told her. It's BEEN dark and I'm out here waiting on you. Pacing."

"Tawana, I swear we gone get caught."

She lit another cigarette.

There she goes again on that we-gone-get-caught shit. She's even smoking more cigarettes the last few days, chain-smoking back to back. I didn't have clue why she thought *she* would get caught any way. All I wanted from her was my shovel I had her to hide. I had watched too many of those crime shows to get caught because I ran over to the local home supply store and now they see me on camera buying a shovel and some damn gloves. That's the only reason I called her scary ass over here to bring it to me. She was the only one I could trust besides my mother. And I hadn't even gotten the guts to tell her what I had done yet. By her being sick that would make her sicker, knowing that here I was back in the same situation *again*. Well, almost the same situation. Lamille was my best friend so I trusted her to help me; Even if it was just hiding a shovel. I needed to make that hole deeper and I wasn't trying to be out by myself at midnight in a dark-ass backyard digging into the earth. Forget the body. Charles was dead. *He* wasn't what I was worried about.

"What I can't understand is, she started the conversation, why did you set him on fire *after* you stabbed him…wasn't he already dead? Don't you think that was going overboard? Because you could've burned down the h-"

"Yeah, well maybe so, but I got mad. Shit." I interrupted.

I saw her looking at me with those big-ass eyes, just the same as Charles used to do when he thought I had said something crazy. I was sick of hearing her try to make sense of it all. It didn't matter now. He tried to bully me again and I killed him. That was the bottom line. Whether I shot him or burned him, all of that didn't matter at this point. That's what I needed her to understand.

It was completely silent for a long while after I said what needed to be said. I felt bad for biting her head off, but it was 11:00 in the middle of the night – 11:32 to be exact- and I really didn't have time for a Q and A, I tried to explain to her. Just shut the fuck up and let me count my steps from the back porch to the big tree in the garden in silence. I had to make this quick. I wanted to hurry up and get this over with.

It took me longer than I thought it would to dig him up because I couldn't find the damn body at first. I had to dig three different holes before I even found it. Then it took what seemed like an hour to make the hole deeper to put him back in it. I had gotten paranoid. I was nervous about having him buried back there, the first place they would look if anybody got suspicious. I had to bury him deeper. No more waiting. It was a good thing I had Tyrone and 'nem coming to pour cement. The yard was all torn up! Besides that it would seem very strange that ain't no body seen him and the yard is all dug up. Let alone the fact that it wasn't a secret how much I despised the man. I guess it would be no different than the fact that

I was about to have a fresh patio in the middle of September instead of worried about my missing ass *dead* husband. Oh well. Ain't no body been to the house in a while so maybe it wouldn't even make a difference.

Every since I married that asshole it seemed like I didn't care about anything anymore. I started enjoying the job I've hated for years just because I was there working 12-hour shifts instead of at home with him. I had gotten to the point of putting Robitussin in his coffee hoping he would fall asleep on his way to work at 5 in the morning. He never even noticed, asking for me to make his coffee as sweet as it was the day before. Do you know I would be disappointed to hear his voice when he called to say he had made it to work? Thinking to myself that he had made it *again*, feeling like I was a failure for not doing something right. I was truly miserable.

"I should have listened to you Mama," I spoke to her as if she was standing next to me. "You knew from the start, didn't you? You never did like Charles. Said you felt the bad spirits whenever he came in the room, holding me back from what was mine because I was always so busy dealing with his crap I couldn't focus on what I shoulda been doing. I should've listened to you Mama. I am sorry. So sorry for not listening to you."

I cried.

That's who I talked to about him the most. I told her just about everything. Of course I didn't tell her about THIS though. Too embarrassed to tell anybody else that it turned out to be a disaster in the making. He was the *one*, as far as the other nurses at work knew. We had a fairytale wedding and they all wished their husbands were true gentlemen like Charles. Of course that is what they *always* said every time I told them a fake-ass story about what I *wish* my marriage was like.

I closed my eyes.

I can try to enjoy life now though. Charles had made sure of that. He wasn't gonna need any of that money he hid in his closet, in his old shoes he didn't know I knew about. He was saving for some old boat to take out on the lake when he went fishing. I can use it for something nice and call it a thank you gift: A thank-you-for-putting-up-with-my-shit gift. Or maybe a hundred thousand dollars worth of gifts, I will say. I deserve that much, don't I? Maybe I could say he went fishing and they couldn't find him after he fell in. He couldn't swim so that *could* happen. Or what about, he finally drank himself to death, like alcohol poisoning or something. No, that won't work either, because where is he? What would I say happened to his body or why didn't I have a funeral? Shit. I didn't know what to say.

"They loved that man." I said out loud, thinking about the two friends he did have. And even one of them was his cousin.

I realized at that very moment that I had not shed one single teardrop over his dead body. I didn't love him at all. I was glad he was gone and I had had three whole days of peace and fucking quiet at my Daddy's house. It was my first Friday in a long while not having to smell the stench of liquor on his hot breath, always ready to pick an argument over simple shit and blame me for the argument just to have a reason to be mad and storm out for hours on end, ignoring my calls. It only took a few times of that crap to realize the game he was playing and I wanted 'IN'. I am quite sure the joke would have been on him if he only knew there was one other person in our fucked up picture who *loved* it when he picked those arguments. Too bad he would never get to know about it. In fact, it was a real downer that he was already laying there covered in blood when I sliced his dick clean off. I don't know why I did that. At the time it felt like it was the final 'fuck you' before I set him on fire.

I smiled to myself, daydreaming about how it was all over. I was lost in knowing that I was no longer a prisoner of my own life and a victim of my own bad decisions. I was a free woman. I was free no matter how I managed to escape my situation.

"You want me to get it Tawana?"

"What?"

"The phone keeps ringing."

I was so deep in thought allowing what I had done to sink in, coming up with lies and making plans for my new future until I didn't even hear my phone ringing. I was covered in mud and soaking wet from all the rain not realizing that it had turned from a sprinkle to a thunderstorm. I had just buried the hatchet and I was filthy. I needed to take a shower and at least wash my hair. I had to sing a solo in church in about 5 hours and I hadn't even gotten out nothing to wear for church yet. I didn't give a shit who was calling.

"Naw don't worry about it. Somebody probably got the wrong number." I reassured her.

Weep What You Sow

Chapter One: Cathy

Who were we to put a question mark where GOD had already put a period? That's the question I would always ask myself when I was watchin' her lay there…dying from that cancer. The big 'C' they call it. It scared me to watch what it can actually do to a person, stripping all the life from you, making you look like a whole 'nother person, losing weight, hair falling out. And it wasn't nothing none of us could do to help her. Even though we needed her here to help with Cobi's baby and to help Justin go all the way through his change, just like that - it was final. It didn't matter how we felt about it. She closed her eyes for good 20 years after Jacob passed away. She was only days away from being on this earth for 59 years. I feel that emptiness from time to time. Can't get it out of my head when I look around here at all the family pictures and how she had the house all fancied up. I didn't change a thing. All I did was come live in it 'cause it was meant to stay in the family. Didn't no body else feel right livin' in it since she was gone. I didn't mind it none. Kinda still felt a piece of her was livin' there too.

The very night she died I called the kids and told them all to get over there, that they mother had gone on. That was the hardest thing I ever had to do besides watching my cousin die right in front of me. Even though it all happened so many years ago it still to this day right now feels like it happened last night! Umph, Lord have mercy!

I remember how all of 'em answered and I had to break the news. I got in touch with all the kids 'cept Tawana. I couldn't get in touch with her for nothing in the world. Jason told me he was about to hang up the phone and book the next flight in and the other two was on they way. Now I knew Tawana worked all those long hours - took after her Mama – a workaholic, they called it, but the girl didn't even answer the phone knowing her Mama could pass on at any moment. Who else gone be calling somebody house that late unless it was an emergency? I never could understand that.

Lord knows Elaine did all she could do for her and the rest of 'em too. After all the help she gave to that oldest chile of hers, the *least* she could've done was be available until the very end. Umph umph umph. We all know as mothers you ain't 'posed to have no favorites, but if she did it was Tawana. Prolly cause she needed the most love and guidance. And Tawana needed her just as much.

I knew it was gonna kill that girl to know that it finally happened, that she took her last breath. I had to send Justin over there to get her so she could see her before they took her away. I called up to that hospital and they told me she didn't have to work that day. I knew she was at the house, probably sitting around drinking and depressed with that Lamille girl. The mousy one. Now that one there was quiet but she drank all the time just like that brother of hers used to do. They was peas in a pod. That downward spiral that Tee took, I blame that girl for all of it 'cause she knew exactly how her brother was and how Tee was too.

It turned into a big show when she finally got over to the house and I knew it was gonna happen just like that when she saw her Mama gone on to the glory there on that bed we had all set up in the living room. Looked like an angel lying there taking a nap. But wasn't no life left in her no more.

When I asked her why she didn't answer none of her phones she claimed she was in deep sleep, that Justin showed up banging on the door and told her she needed to come now was what woke her. I let her know that I had been calling since the minute I saw her Mama take a turn for the worse, struggling to breathe and me sitting up wondering why it was taking so long to catch another breath. If she would've just answered the phone…

"Cathy PLEASE!" She begged me. "Please tell me she ain't dead. I don't know what I'm gonna do without my Mommy!"

She howled and carried on so, crawling around on the floor next to Elaine and holding on to Justin's ankles. She had a lot of what looked to me like dried up mud on her shoes that she was leaving on the carpet as she went from crawling around to sprawled all out like an eagle in the middle of the living room floor. Her hair was all over her head, it smelled like she had drank a whole gallon of liquor. She was a damn mess. I felt sorry for her. At least if she had've answered the phone it could have been a little different for her. I'm sure she would have thrown on a hat. Maybe some clothes, too, not just an overcoat. She was butt-naked under that coat, crawling around on the floor, whimpering and begging Elaine to come back from the dead.

That's when I really wished Jason lived here in town. For some reason or another he had a way with Tawana. She listened to him. If she didn't listen to anybody else she cared about what he thought and listened to his directions. He surely wouldn't have stood for any of that kind of behavior and neither would Mick if he was there. Jason was always telling her how she ruining the family's reputation. It worked a lot of the time. He was a doctor in North Carolina. Worked at a health center there, helping out in the community.

"Tawana! Please, honey. It will be ok. She is better now, not suffering baby. You are gonna ruin all our reputations." Justin pleaded with his older sister.

He was irritated. He threw that Michael Kors 'suitcase' on the coffee table and I swore the legs was gonna crumble from underneath it. He unzipped that bag like it had made him angry.

"You want people to start talking about the good doctor's family? Them old folk at that church?"

He found what he had been digging 'round in there for because he snatched it out like it was a small pistol and he was about to put her out of her misery.

"Are you *trying* to prove them right about us all these years honey? Rolling around that floor like some sick puppy dog. You a NURSE baby. Please get your tail up off that floor. Girl just stop! *Stop it.*"

He turned and walked away, hand in the air totally dismissing that tantrum. I couldn't believe it. It was as if Jason had come to life in Justin. The quiet one. He never did say too much but he put Tawana in her place all whilst putting the Sephora gloss across his lips.

The coroner was standing there taking it all in. It was obvious that the little man did not want to add any more fuel to this fire bomb by putting Elaine on the gurney. There was further no way in hell she was going in no body bag with everybody looking and mourning over her. Jacobi was standing there with her mouth open letting the baby cry her little eyes out. She wasn't doing a thing to comfort that baby. The baby was crying because that was her Granny laying there not moving and the poor thang didn't know what was going on. She just knew something wasn't right about it. Everybody had just come loose from the seams when I looked around that room. Justin had finally collapsed at the dining room table crying into his hands and Tawana was still whimpering but had sat up in the corner, huddled up in that old coat.

"This is all too much for me right now today!" I took the baby. "Hush, chile, Cat got you. Jacobi, hand me that bottle," I ordered her. "We have enough to contend with right now. Sir, please go on and do your job and we can deal with this. Come on baby. Cobi, Justin, y'all get up and come on with me. Up the stairs, each one of you. Tawana, get on up and come on upstairs too. Get on out the way so the man can do what he need to do."

Just like six-year-olds, they climbed the steps slowly, all of 'em. I was finally able to say my good-bye to my favorite cousin in the peace and quiet. The coroner stood silently by the door patiently waiting on me as I kissed her cheek. I was whispering to myself how I was there with her through her sickness until the sound of the zipper 'cause I couldn't believe it myself that it had finally came about, her dying like that. He was wheelin' her off to them so they could prod around and find out why her body had finally given up.

That whole while I was with her. Going to all them doctors when they was trying to figure out what was going on too. It was all over with. The sound of the zipper on that body bag echoed through that living room and down the walk for weeks, months after the service.

Jason and his new wife flew in the day after it all happened. I know the kids were all so glad to see him. I was especially glad to see him. That boy had been through some hard times hisself and managed to keep a level head on his shoulders. Lucky he didn't have no tight relationship with his daddy 'cause him being locked away and his mama and Elaine passing on to glory sho nuff would've been too much for him to handle.

Ole' Larry wrote to him ev'ry now and again to remind him just how proud he was for having that good life he was livin'. My guess is that he wanted to apologize about how for getting hisself right back in trouble too. Now that was an awful shame to go back to prison after doing all them years in there. He gave up the rights of seeing his oldest child doing as good as Jason was! I guess he figured it couldn't be helped what he had to do since he missed out on being a parent for Jason. Umph umph umph. I don't know.

When I talked to Jason all he said was that he felt he owed Larry something at least for giving him life. That's all he ever said on the matter. Least to me. Guess he did forgive his daddy for taking his mother away from him at such a young age. He never did have to fend for hisself that's for sure. He had Elaine's guidance and Mick's too. Now look at him – he a doctor. That's a hell of an accomplishment. He went on and got married to a lady he met working in that clinic. Sharon was a social worker that helped the patients find insurance and services to get food and transportation. She was about to have a baby for him. A boy. I was happy for him. So smart. He kept in touch with them other ones, he ain't leave 'em behind and forget they exist like he coulda did. After all they wasn't his blood sisters and brother. Elaine had just raised him up that way. It seemed easier, you know? He went from calling her Auntie to Mama after a while. And that was perfectly ok with her.

Elaine instilled them same values in all of 'em, to be a family and stick together. They all been through some changes but they got through 'em together just keeping all that in mind. Helping each other out the way they did. I made it my duty to talk to the chil'ren as often as I could too. We had a rapport I must say that. They all was special in they own ways.

All them beautiful flowers in all colors decorated the entire church. Looked to me like half the city was there to pay respect at the service. Folk prolly believed it was all for some celebrity in Georgia, the way it was all packed up like that. And I don't know how she did it, but Tawana sang a real pretty song for her mama and got through the whole thing without crying out. Mick gave the eulogy for her and talked about how she was sent back to her maker so she could be repaired. It was a very nice service. Not a dry eye showed up. She sure was loved.

A special lady that cousin of mine. She had the whole service planned out a whole year before she passed on. The funeral program was written up and she picked out her own casket. She had done it all before she got down too sick to comb her own hair. Turned out just how she planned it.

It had been years since her death, I thought to myself with a deep sigh. Hell, some church folk still to this day saying she took secrets with her. Saying she died to keep Tawana from going to jail because she loved her just that much. You know if Elaine confessed and there was no way to prove it wasn't her that did it, that was going to get Tawana off the hook. How could she make her own self die from cancer?

Folks come up with all kinds of nonsense. I heard something about it being a chemtrail that was responsible for all the dysfunction and diseases people was suffering from. The murdering and the homosexuality. Even the drinking and drugs people got theyselves involved in was supposed to be a conspiracy from the government to get rid of all us black folk. I had never heard of such a thing! Said it was making men want to be with other men and dress up like women. If that didn't beat all! What chemical did the government have that could do something like that? You mean to tell me jets could fly over Georgia and change us into zombies?

That must be some strong potion the government had if that was the truth. Guess it would have to be for them to change people into something other else. Umph. I can't believe that it was some talk about Elaine dying just so she could help Tawana get out of the mess she was in! I declare! To think she died to keep her daughter from being the blame in a murder? The bottom line was Elaine had been dead for years and can't no body go in after her to put her in prison for no murder. That chapter was over.

Chapter 2: Jacobi

The only thing Mama could think to do was lean on the church after me and Justin's real dad died. Daddy's church - Greater St. Mary Baptist Church. That included us right along with her. Every Sunday. Then going every Sunday wasn't good enough it turned into going to Sunday school too. Then every Wednesday there we were in Bible Study. I hated that more than going to Sunday school. All the other kids in the neighborhood got to come home from school and go outside and play, but we couldn't do that on no Wednesday. We had to come home and change our clothes to go to church. I felt like some damn Mormon or something. I thought I was gonna pull my hair out when she volunteered me and Justin to sing in that youth choir. Choir rehearsal was on a damn Thursday! It wasn't like it was a bad thing to be in church, but it seemed like we were being punished for something because we was always there. It made me almost hate being a Christian.

Me and Justin was always trying to spend the night at Tawana's on the weekends so we didn't have to go to that boring church. We couldn't always go because she had to work some weekends. That's when we HAD to go. Good thing me and Justin was in the same class. At least we had each other to talk to. Them other kids were way different than us. I think they wanted to be there, sitting there paying attention to the Sunday school teacher. Not us. All we was thinking about was when would be a good time to sneak the hell out of there. Didn't no body care about what she was talking about! It didn't even make no sense! Justin used to tell her it didn't make sense and tell her to explain it. If he still didn't get it he would ask her to explain it another way. She used to get so mad at him! Back then he was just getting started. Him sitting up there acting silly was the only way we got through church. Sitting up there talking 'bout folks and laughing at what Sister Christine was wearing or counting all the big-ass hats on the Mothers' board pews.

We did all kinda stuff during church we ain't have no business doing like sneaking out going to the corner store. Didn't none of them nerdy-ass kids ever wanna walk around there with us but always wanted a piece of our stuff. I wasn't *giving* them shit. I sold it to them. Now and Laters and Tootsie Rolls was 5 for a quarter. I sold the Lemonheads and Red Hots – the box candy- for a quarter. You should've seen them giving us all that change they was supposed to put in the offering plate. We sold so much candy on Sundays it became our hustle.

Right after Devotion we snuck out so we could go around the corner to the store. People was still getting there around that time so no body even noticed we were gone. If they did know we never got in trouble so they couldn't have told on us. They probably expected us to be bad in the first place. Up in there doing whatever we wanted because it was our daddy's church. Everybody knows the worse kids in the church house is the Pastor's kids. I think that's how it is in all the black churches. Probably 'cause they always had to be there. It drove all of us to be bad.

I had a big crush on this boy named Todd. He was only in me and Justin's Sunday school class at first, but his mom made him join the youth choir too. He wasn't like them other kids in church. He was pretty cool. He didn't like being at church no more than we did. He was actually normal. We didn't mind him hanging around with us. Todd was the one who got everybody's candy orders when we were selling candy. He would go around the balcony and write down what they wanted. That was our system on Sundays. Jay gave him free candy for his help. I had a crush on him so I didn't mind giving him candy whether he helped or not. He was cute. One time Justin stood guard in front of the door after Sunday School so I could kiss him. It was just a peck on the lips, but he was mine after that. That made us boyfriend and girlfriend, I decided. My first boyfriend.

"I really liked him. I really liked Todd." I reminisced.

"You STILL blaming me for that Cobi? For real? Neither one of us knew. At least you didn't have sex with the little boy. He used both of us really." My brother schooled me. "BOTH our asses got played."

"I *AM* still mad about Todd, Jay!" I chuckled. "You KNEW I really liked that boy! I can laugh about it now because we was kids." I took a drag of my cigarette. I asked him flat out one day 'Why you keep asking me all them questions about my brother?' I was mad that he wanted to know if you liked boys. I was protective of you, shit. I knew you were different, how you always wanted to put on Tawana's clothes and trying on Mama's shoes and shit. Shit your skin has always *been* perfect, but I started paying closer attention when your lips was all shiny and shit all the time."

"That was how I wanted to see myself Miss Cobi. That's what *I* wanted to see when *I* looked in the mirror. I wanted to be '*pretty*' and have pretty things. I didn't want to play no football and basketball. Just because I'm tall I'm supposed to tackle people or throw some damn ball in a hoop? That's dumb as hell. I'm gonna take these size 11 feet and put them in a nice pair of pumps and use these long arms to carry a big-ass bag! That's what Jay the Greatest Bitch ever is gonna do, *ok*?"

"I accepted it baby brother. Of course I accepted whatever *you* did but *he* didn't have no right to be asking about you. He was *my* boyfriend, always wanting you to hang with us. Checking you out."

Justin started calling himself Jay when he was around 13 or 14. I asked why he didn't want to be called Justin and he said it was like me being called Jack or Jim. A 'J' could be talking about any person, a boy or a girl, he told me. He didn't want to be labeled under a boy name like Justin anymore. I ain't never heard of no girls named Justin so he had a point. I understood why he wanted to be Jay after he put it like that even though I still called him Justin at times. Hell. He was Justin for most of our lives so it was hard not to. I called him Jay sometimes and other times he was Justin. It didn't bother him none.

Everything about my brother was changing right in front of my eyes. This new person named Jay even had a different voice than the Justin I was used to hearing. All of a sudden his voice sounded like that man's who did Mama's hair and the manager at the Chicken Shack. They all sounded the same for some reason. I could only explain it as how my grandmother would sound if she had a man's voice. Whether she was making you laugh or cry, she had the same sing-song voice. Jay sounded like that when he was telling one of his jokes or putting you in your place just like her. This new Jay I had in my life would show up in a nice dress with all the matching accessories or come downstairs in a pair of jeans and a sweater. It was always a surprise with him.

Todd never acted like he was like that. I knew it though. My so-called boyfriend was in love with my brother. I had a feeling Jay had a crush on him, too. Sitting there smiling every time I told him my man asked about him *again*.

"What's so funny about that? Why you smiling?" I used to want to know. "You like him or something? Justin? You like my *boy*friend?"

Wasn't nothin' funny about him asking about my little brother all the time!

"I'm going to tell Mama about you skipping school if you don't tell me. You better tell me something Jay."

I was mad at first. There was no way people couldn't see Jay was different. If Todd keep asking about him he must like him then ain't no body stupid! We only saw each other at church anyway. I kissed that boy way back when I was 13! Years ago! If they like each other they can *have* each other. I pouted. Fuck Todd. I told Justin it's too many other boys. I wasn't bout to fight over no one boy. Especially if he liked my brother more than me. Todd thought it was a secret that Justin was sucking his dick in the basement at church. Jay promised he wouldn't tell but he told me! As close as we was he *better* tell me! Jay told me everything. I knew about the basement and all about the first time he let Todd screw him, not wanting him to wear a rubber and how Todd came real quick after he got it in. He was in love with Jay! And Jay felt the same exact way.

It went on for I don't know how many years. That boy was buying him stuff, giving him money. All he did was beg to meet him somewhere. Sneaking around all the time. Sex was always on Todd's agenda. That's all they did when they got together. It was a big secret because he didn't want no body to know he was gay. He said he wasn't. Still talking all hard and fighting people for disrespecting him but he was dating a boy. That's probably why he was always giving Jay money. To keep him happy so *he* wouldn't tell.

When that girl popped up at our house with his cell phone and told Jay she was Todd's baby mama and they had a 3-year-old daughter we couldn't believe it! She said they had been together since she was in junior high school and she didn't know he was gay. She was crying bad! Her name was Cassie. She had the baby when she in the 11th grade so her parents were upset with her about that she told us soon as she came in. The fact that the baby was with Todd was more unacceptable especially to her dad.

Cassie said Todd was known as a thug on the south side and that her dad couldn't stand him. She was so hurt she told us everything about Todd and everything about her life too. Crying the whole time. She wanted to go to college and graduate and get a good job. All that had changed because of messing around with Todd. Her parents wanted more from her and all she wanted was to be with Todd she cried out. That was why her whole family hated him. Well apparently they hated him because he hit on her too. All that and she still stayed with him.

My whole shoulder was wet because she was crying on my shoulder. You could tell she was still young and didn't know too much about being with a dude like Todd. Just from the stuff she was telling us he controlled her every move. He probably told her where to go and where not to go. Probably any place he was meeting Jay was where he told her she couldn't go. Obviously she did whatever he said because she was all in love with him. That's why I didn't think it was a good idea to tell her all that stuff when she started asking questions. She wanted details. That girl wanted to know when they met and what they did when they hooked up. She was asking Jay *how* they did it.

"That's how we be doing it, are you ***SERIOUS***?"

Cassie had a head on her shoulders we found out 'cause she got the details off the picture and found out when he took it and the area he was in when it was taken. That girl drove around looking for Mama's green Escalade because he was posing in front of a green truck in the picture. Come to find out she had gone through his phone while he was sleep and saw a picture of Jay in front of our house and couldn't understand why Todd would have a picture of a man wearing makeup, dressed like that. A gay man's picture in his phone? She needed to get to the bottom of it. There was no way that she was in this situation. This was a dream. Her baby daddy couldn't be dating the beautiful man in the picture. And in the picture she saw my brother was on point! Had on the knee-high boots and duck lips with the purple lipstick.

She was damn lucky my brother wasn't one of them nasty people sleeping with a bunch of other people. She should've been thanking her lucky stars that she only found out he was gay and not gay with some disease she wouldn't be able to get rid of. That shit happens all the time only instead of finding out the dude gay you find out 'cause you done went to the doctor sick. Then find out you got HIV or something. She better be glad about that instead then. He didn't use no condom with Cassie *or* Jay. He nasty! What if one of them did have something? It was too much to hear about. They were comparing notes! Why the fuck were they comparing notes? She was out of control by then. Jay was getting upset too. Neither one of them knew he was messing with somebody else. Not using nothing. They both trusted him.

Something just kept telling me she shouldn't know this much about my brother and his relationship with that boy. Todd would never admit to NO BODY that he was fucking a dude. A gay south side gang member. That was about to be all *over* Facebook. I pulled Jay to the side and told him I didn't want him to be a target for exposing that boy. She did have every right to know her baby's daddy was gay, but damn. Was this the only way? Couldn't she just say she saw the picture so it was obvious? Why did Jay have to be the one to tell her that?

I guess it was already happening. The cat was out of the bag and Jay opened the bag when she knocked on our door. She was sitting on our couch so she suspected it and found *him* though. If it wasn't my brother it was going to be somebody so she needed confirmation, I reasoned with myself. This needed to be told. Todd was having sex with Jay. He *loved* being with my brother. She needed to know. I felt bad for her that her little family had been broken up with a sledge hammer. She showed us pictures of all three of them together at the park and at their apartment being a little family. That little girl looked just like his ass too. They made a cute family I ain't gonna lie. His punk ass had two whole different lives. One with her and the baby and one with my brother.

She got her confirmation. Jay had been in the picture for longer than they had been together. He told her how long they had been messing around and about all that money. That asshole spent more money on Justin than he did on his own daughter.

"You can give up $400 because you getting your dick sucked and fucking your little boyfriend 3 and 4 times a week, but can't give me $100 for Kara?" She asked the air.

She left after that. We was still in the door staring behind her car, she sped off so fast. We didn't know what to expect. What the hell was she about to go do? I know she ain't about to put a hit out on us. We ain't know about that girl. This all on Todd ass for not being honest. The first thing she gone do is go and get up in his face and tell him she found out he gay. After that I know she gone tell all his friends on the south side and Facebook about how she met Jay and what they been doing all these years. Watch. Damn that's messed up. He gone be so embarrassed I wouldn't be surprised if he killed hisself.

"This ain't over," I warned my baby brother.

He knew too. All he could do was nod.

"He about to call and cuss me *out*." He waited for the phone.

I didn't think he was gonna call. What was he gonna say? He had lied to Jay a million times too, talking about he wanted to be with him forever. Ha! That was some bullshit. He couldn't even admit he was *gay*, let alone MARRY him. That was some heat-of-the-moment shit. Some it-feels-so-good-so-I'm-talking-shit promise.

Something was about to happen and I was scared. We ended up having to tell Mama 'cause it had gotten serious. I didn't know where to start and he didn't know where to start either. The only thing she ever knew about Todd was that he was the little boy from church that *I* useta like. Ain't no body want her to know about me letting Jay have him and how it had been a whole 4 years that Jay was doing it with him. She didn't need to know my brother was having sex. Not because he was gay but because I know she would feel like he was too young to be having sex with *any*body, Todd or not. He was still her big baby.

"Just tell her Justin," I made him confess. "We gotta tell her what's going on just in case."

She was calm about it. We ended up telling her everything. The whole story. At first we just told her that Jay was messing with this boy and we found out he had a girlfriend – how mad she was when she came over and met him. How she didn't even know her man was that way. We expected her to go off and she didn't even get mad. He kept telling her more and more and she was taking it better than what we both thought she would. She was actually cool about it. She didn't even yell at Jay. By the time he got to the part about Todd having a girlfriend, I let her know that Jay didn't have no idea about that girl or know about no baby either.

"Her name is Cassie, Mama, and they been together for a long time. They even got a baby together, live together and the whole thing. But he out here messing around with Justin."

"Cassie?"

"Yeah she said her name Cassie. Cassandra. We don't know her last name. But she Todd's baby mama and he was dating both of them at the same time – Mama you ain't mad? Ain't that a trip?"

"It's a trip alright."

"Mama it don't bother you 'bout him trying to get back at me? Well at Jay, but if he come at him then I - "

"He better not come to THIS house. And if he know what's good for him, he bet not bother you neither. I wouldn't worry about it. Todd got his own problems now. His baby's mother just found out he ain't who he said he was. He ain't got no time to be trying to get no revenge."

Her theory was if you stay ready you don't ever have to get ready for anything. She meant every word of it too. That's why she wasn't fazed. If Todd even thought about putting his finger on our doorbell I am sure that little lady would've found a way to say he broke in and she had to kill him! That would show him! Who did he think he was? He wasn't no match for Elaine!

I was dreaming though. It wasn't gonna happen like that. Somebody was gonna pay for the whole city finding out he had all that shit in the closet with him. Why *wouldn't* he take it out on Jay? Jay was the one who got him out the closet and he was gonna try to kill him I bet. I was gonna have to have my brother's back he was definitely not all by hisself. That meant both of us needed to be prepared for whatever was going down next. We wasn't worried about shit happening at our house 'cause Mama was there and she was way better than having a big ass gun. I was scared about him catching us out at the mall or hell, at church somewhere.

"Look what I got," I showed him the guns. "I got some bullets for them too. We need these Justin. All jokes aside."

"Girl if Mama knew you had them guns in here she would kill me and you. Neither one of us know how to use no gun girl!"

"I know but we need to learn how. This serious. You can't be exposing no body like that. I'm scared. You need to be scared too, why you sitting there saying we don't need no gun!"

"I am scared girl. I know how that boy is better than anybody, but guns is dangerous as hell girl. You think we need a gun? What about some pepper spray instead. Then we can beat his ass to death while he can't see. Pepper spray will -"

"Fuck some damn pepper spray. What if we don't see him coming? That's dumb. Telling that girl just started a war Justin. We gotta watch our backs."

"That girl probably at home giving him a piece of her mind. And he got a mean streak in him. I bet he jumping on her right now honey. Even though he the one wrong. He get mad at you for knowing he wrong. I almost had to let him know that there is a man in here honey and he can't do me like that, like some battered woman. I had to go 'bass' on that little ass. I had to go 'bass' a few times as a matter of fact."

"What you mean go 'bass'? I ain't never heard that before. What is *that*?"

"I had to put the *bass* back in my voice Jacobi. Wake up darling. I had to work at this gaycent I have, honey, my *pretty* voice. I wasn't born with it. I can summon that man that's in here. I had to go bass to back his little ass up."

"Well then you know you need it. Here. Take this one."

He never called or nothing. We went to the gun range and did all that learning how to use them guns and we never even seen him no more. I was expecting him to call Jay's cell phone that same day Cassie popped up. She left around 4:00 or something like that so I thought for sure he was gonna call him but he didn't. If I was him I would've called Jay as soon as we got done arguing. I would have at least called to dog him about all the stuff my girl found out. He knew Jay had to have told her their business. Wasn't no other way she could know all that.

7:30.

No call. Next thing you know it was midnight. He didn't call. When Jay called his phone it went right to voicemail. He must've just turned it off, all them calls he was probably getting about what Cassie put on her page. She got on Facebook and didn't leave shit out. She posted all the pictures that was in his phone so it wasn't like he could deny it to no body. She tagged Justin, Todd people, and some other girl named Octavia. I don't know who that girl was. Maybe somebody else she found out about. A big ass mess.

Todd wasn't on Facebook no more though. His whole profile was deleted so he had no idea she did all that. I don't know if he deleted it or if Cassie did but either way, he had to be embarrassed as hell. Everybody knew what he was on so I can imagine what would've been said on there if he did have his page. All that lying so he could have his cake and eat it too and he ended up losing *both* of them anyway. Wasn't no fixing *that*. How *could* he fix it?

Cassie made a live video screaming about kicking him out and you could see him in the background. He was getting his stuff out of drawers the whole time and he didn't say anything to her. Didn't try to deny it or nothing. Cassie's last post about Justin was something about him being free to go be with whatever dude he wanted to because it was over between them. She made sure she said he wasn't never seeing his daughter no more. Her video was the last images of him.

Todd disappeared into thin air behind it all. It had been weeks since Cassie kicked him out. His car was still parked at the apartment. He didn't try to call her or his mama. It was obvious he was already moving out so why didn't he finish getting it and leave instead of leave the shit there like that? Now we all thought something happened to him. He left all his stuff in the car and vanished. What was so weird about the whole thing is that his mom – and Cassie – said his wallet and high blood pressure medicine was in the glove compartment. His toothbrush and brush, all his cologne -in the front seat.

Weeks passed. No body had seen him. He didn't reach out to Jay, he didn't try to contact Cassie trying to get back in with her either. His mama didn't know what else to do. She had made the missing person report and posters. The phone was off so the police couldn't track him that way. Wasn't nothing to do except wait to see if he would come back.

After a month or so his car was *still* sitting there. Where could that boy have gone and he didn't have a car or wallet? It didn't make no sense that somebody came and got him and he didn't at least take his license and some money. Anything could have happened to him. Or maybe he killed hisself out of embarrassment.

His phone stopped going to voicemail after a while. The message let everybody calling know the number was no longer in service. That's really when everybody started that "Find Todd' stuff. After being gone for 6 months without a single trace you can tell that didn't no body care about him being gay. They just wanted to find him. It wasn't cool to find out he was like that but it wasn't so bad that he had to just disappear. That's what his friend Tommy put on Facebook. Everybody was writing on Tommy's page and sharing pictures of him. We all wanted to find him alive. We forgot all about thinking he was going to do something to us. Even Justin was on there posting stuff. It was our fault for telling Cassie about him in the first place.

He was missing for a real long time. It was like almost a year or something like that. I just remember that it had died down for a while and then they started reporting a body had been discovered by a construction crew downtown. I guess they had to do an autopsy and all that and identify who it was before they could say anything else. That's how we finally found out Todd was gone for real. It was all over. It was him they found down there. They identified the clothes at the scene - the same clothes he had on in Cassie's live video: that yellow shirt with the '3' on it and jeans. Positively identified him from those teeth after that. Them gold teeth and that gap he had. Somebody killed that boy. Somebody killed him and put him behind that building.

When they started construction down there for them new condominiums they were advertising as 'coming soon' they dug him up. That man told the reporter they were tearing that building down and digging around when they saw clothes. And there was the smell. The strong dead body smell. I heard dead bodies got a real bad smell. If they never decided to buy that warehouse Todd would've never been found like that. Ain't nothing else down there so no body would've been down there to smell that.

Wasn't too much information on the news when it first came out they found him. Todd's family and of course his mom was demanding answers. When they tried to investigate his death to see what happened it was all over town how Todd was just a body. I didn't understand what they were trying to say, that he was just a 'body'. Like what were they talking about? That he was gone? Dead? That's what I thought they meant. But they wasn't saying that. The coroner who looks at murders like that, or whatever the circumstances were about him said that he didn't have nothing in his body. He didn't have no heart, his lungs were gone, his kidneys. Everything. He didn't even have eyes. He was empty or something.

The detective said he was downtown in an abandoned field so more than likely it was an animal that got to him. A coyote or a wolf? How could an animal like that carefully choose his eyes and the insides of his body without tearing him into pieces?

It felt like it wasn't real. Like a real bad dream. I couldn't even think about something like that happening. No body had no answers about it. After they got down questioning people and doing all that investigating, them detectives closed the case. They found out who had something to do with it. I couldn't believe it at first. Cassie's dad ended up getting arrested for that.

"You remember this picture?" I showed him a picture of all of us at church. Me, him, and Todd with Pops by the alter at Greater St. Mary's. We was still kids.

"Yeah," He took it, staring at it for I don't know how long. Jay's nails were perfect! I noticed.

"Todd was my first boythang. I do kinda miss him girl. After all these years. Mama didn't feel bad about shit neither did she Cobi? Never said two words about it. Not two damn words about Todd little ass."

"Naw she ain't feel bad about nothing. He ain't have no business doing what he did. You can't be running around here playing no body like that. You feel bad 'bout what happened?"

"I do for that baby. Her daddy gone. Poor thang ain't got no daddy now."

"Well Mama was a protector Jay, that's what she said she was here for. For *us*. To make
sure we were never in harm's way. That woman didn't play when it came to any of us you know that. Whatever she had to do."

"I know."

Chapter 3: The Closet

Everybody and they mama used to talk about we must've been raised fucked up since he had turned out that way but that ain't have nothing to do with how we was raised. Yeah he WAS gay, but Jay always did wanna be just like Mama. He loved her to death! That's not why he was gay though. He loved men and the woman he admired was who he modeled himself after. It wasn't the other way around. Don't that make sense? It did to me. Ain't no body in our family judge him. That was Jay. That was how he was. We didn't know him no different way. All his style was just like our mother. *ALL* Elaine. What *man* you know can put on a pair of skinny jeans with a pair of high-heeled boots, grab a big ass purse and be *fabulous*?

"Don't no body like no wet clothes, he fussed at me. "No Miss *Jacobi*, put that cornstarch under them rolls and titties. Sprinkle some in between them legs be*fore* you put ya clothes on. Thatta get rid of them sweat rings. Listen to what I'm telling ya."

I couldn't believe it when he told me to use that cornstarch outta Mama's kitchen cabinet like baby powder. It worked like a charm. The chair wasn't wet no more when I got up. Useta be so embarrassed in the summertime getting up from a chair and you could see my big 'ole butt print still sitting in the same spot! Been using it ever since. It worked. When that ain't happen no more I started listening to all his advice and it all worked.

Years later I was shopping at the grocery store for my beauty products. Anything Jay told me I had to try it. People need to recognize. Ain't the shit you buy in the mall that work the best. Be the natural products. All the stuff that be right there in your mama's cabinet.

Turn left down aisle 3, box of cornstarch, right turn down the laxative section for the milk of magnesia and the castor oil. The milk of magnesia is my primer. I used that to make a palette so I can stay matte all day. Jay told me to put my foundation right over that chalky face when it dry. The plain kind, not cherry! Oh, and I need my Vicks Vaporub to put in my hair...he says that opens my pores so my hair will grow. I gotta admit your head do be tingling so I figured it was busy opening pores. Felt just like how it feels when you chew a piece of double mint gum. I could feel my head *breathing.*

Using that stuff and putting castor oil in my hair worked for real. I don't even use grease. I use castor oil to grow my eyebrows and hair and I use that Vicks too. It sure did grow hair! Justin wrote a book 'bout all them beauty secrets. People was buying it and they was all doing the same thing. He would do hair in our basement and had all them ladies using that stuff. All of 'em was using castor oil and mixing stuff up like potions in spray bottles. That's how he decided what he wanted to do. He was good at doing hair. All them beauty secrets he had...he already had a buncha customers. Why not gone 'head and open a real shop?

Mama ended up selling everything as far as the business – the equipment, the land we owned – well some of it, and she split all the money between all of us. It was a *lot.* At the time we was still young, me and Jay was- so our part of it had to go in some account until we turned 25. Mama felt that by that age we would've decided on what we really wanted to do in life and that money could help us be 'grounded', she said. When he decided to have a beauty shop with his money Pops helped him pick out a real nice building. It was called The Wild Hair. I came up with the name for him. Pops had some contractors that was sweet with designing help out and told them to spare no expense. It was definitely one of a kind.

Jay had that shop laid *out.* He had pictures of Mama, Daddy, and Tawana hanging up in the lobby in big gold frames. It was supposed to be like a family shop so he made sure he had pictures of everybody hanging up. Our pictures, one of me and Kennedy, Pops and Jason and his wife, were hanging up too, but he didn't have ours as big as theirs was. That was cool with me since that was a kinda memorial thing for him.

It was a one-stop shop. I was so proud of him! It had a cafeteria in the lower level. You could go in there and order whatever you wanted from the grill. It was a couple people down there that did all the cooking for him. It was a cafeteria like in the hospital. You know how you can go in and get something cooked up or it was stuff on the menu for that day you could buy. Or if you just wanted to grab a bag of chips and a pop, you could do that too. That's how it was in there. The Wild Eatery. Then on the next level was where you got your hair washed and conditioned, dyed - all that stuff. Upstairs, now that was the top level. That was the final step. That's the floor where you got your masterpiece. The finished product.

Jay's shop was really popular. It was right on the corner of Grandolph and Henthorne Parkway, down the street from the mall. Everybody went to that mall so it wasn't hard to miss, how it was designed and how many cars were always in the lot. The shop was just as popular as the mall in fact. The only shop in Georgia that had a cafeteria and believe it or not a child care center in the lower level. That came after the fact. That idea was born right after the Bebe kids broke a $2000 massage chair. When that happened and a week later some dumb girl got arrested for leaving her baby in a hot car 'cause she was getting her hair done, that was another idea. A child care room. For $10 an hour the ladies could have a Red Cross Certified babysitter take care of the kids *including* feeding them.

When we got that going that attracted more people to get their heads done. A lot of 'em never went nowhere 'cause they had bad kids. Wasn't no way they was bringing no kid to no beauty shop. That changed for them.

The appointments were booked out for months. It went from him and Monroe being the only stylists to him adding 3 more. Monroe came up with hiring some girls right out of hair school to work on the first level. Wasn't no harm in doing that, not too much experience needed to work down there doing all the shampooing and dyeing customers. Stylist *and* barbers up in there. Jay was making money hand over fist, charging $300 for braids and for a good weave with Bohyme human hair supplied by the Wild Hair. Even that hairdo *started* at $200.

Between him and Jason's careers, hearing all those stories and knowing how much money I could make working with one of them compared to my paychecks every week, I didn't know if I should get into the hair business or go up there where Jason was and take him up on his offer to work at the clinic. Money wasn't exactly the issue, but there was things I wanted and I wasn't getting them on my salary. I would *have* to go into my account. I didn't want to do that. Anything could happen and I didn't want to spend my money on every little thing Cobi wanted. That was why I was working at that boring ass job every day, but I was sick of it! Change is always a good thing, Tawana used to always tell me. She was spontaneous and it was nothing for her to make her mind up and it was done! That is how I wanted to be too. With everything including my career.

"Hey little sis," He always called me that. "You know you can always come and work in my practice. Mom would look down on you and smile if you did. Maybe even brag on you a little more than she did Tawana," Jason would joke. "The world needs more of us."

I wanted to be a teacher back then so I used some of my money and went to school. I got my Bachelors of Education but Jason wanted me to go back to school to be an NP. Nurse Practitioner. If I did that, he tried to convince me, I could be his partner at the clinic he ran. It could be OUR practice, he always bragged. Brother and sister. We could take over Public Health. We could have a clinic that had a dental clinic, family medicine providers, a prenatal department... we could expand! He dreamed. We could get a grant, he assured. It sounded cool, don't get me wrong. I would love to be up there with Jason. I missed him so much, but I just wasn't willing to go back to school. I had done that already. I was fine with being Miss. Cobi to all my little kids for at least a little while. That's what Justin called me too.

Miss Cobi. The tallest person in the room. I was teaching 5 and 6 year olds how to spell their names and coloring all day. Singing the alphabet and tracing letters. For 3 years I did that. It was a decent career but it was boring. Mama would've been proud of me for having a career and not just a job since I had Kennedy to take care of. I needed more for us though. It wasn't enough. I needed to find my mojo!

The highlight of my days was listening to all the shit Jay had going on in that shop! Who was fucking who and what sale was going on at the mall. That was more interesting than what I heard about all day: Peanut butter and jelly sandwiches or pet frogs. Something had to give. Dealing with Michael's ass at night and then up to go to work day in and day out. Talking to Mama and Tawana about what would be the best for me. I needed to be with my baby brother on a regular basis, I finally made up my mind. Not just on the phone.

It did help my decision a little bit to hear him talk about all the money he was bringing in and see all that popularity he had! That boy had every bag that came out and every Michael Kors anything that was in existence. He spoiled the shit outta Kennedy. My baby even had watches. I wanted a piece of that action.

After 1,500 hours of cosmetology school and 13 months of cutting and curling old women at Hair Plus Cosmetology College, I had a certificate that was going to help me change my circumstances. Working all them hours next to my brother, named as the best stylist in Georgia hands down, I was doing almost as many weaves as he was after a few months! Especially after he let everybody know I was his sister. My mojo was in FULL effect!

I bought that silver Infinity Q60 I had always wanted with my rewards. I had my groove: An engagement ring on my finger that was shining like the North Star, a 'For Sale' sign in my yard that needed to come down because it had just been sold, and a smile on my face that seemed permanent. I know I shoulda known better. Shit don't never work out like that. I knew there was going to be a catch to it somewhere.

I was on my last customer for the evening. All my clients had been relaxed, dyed and cut and it was time for me to go. They were satisfied and so was I that another work day had come and gone. No more weaves, no more braids, this girl was tired. Mike had plans to go out of town to look in on his grandmother and that was fine by me. I didn't want to be bothered any way. I had to pick Kennedy up from her piano lesson and then I was going straight home. I didn't even feel like stopping for gas!

"We are ordering pizza!" I let her know in advance as soon as she threw her book bag in the backseat.

She looked at me like I was crazy. I guess it was the first thing that came out of my mouth. But that meant I'm tired and don't even *ask* me to stop for anything. I ain't stopping at McDonalds, don't ask me to cook shit- I ain't even stopping to pick the *pizza* up I was so beat. I'll order it and they can *deliver* it to me. It is lazy, I thought, as I drove right past Marcos. But whatever, I argued with myself. I will tip them, I justified. I'm tired. My feet hurt, wearing some new shoes I just got. They wasn't broke in enough to be in them all day, standing there doing some braids.

I had made it all the way home when I realized: I never did get the money out of the register for Kennedy's school tuition. That was due no later than Thursday morning. Tomorrow. I forgot the money *and* the perm to do her hair. Damn. I ain't have no other choice but to go back to the shop. It was gonna take another 30 minutes to get way back up there from my house. Damn, I thought, doing a 360.

"What is his car doin' up here? He should've been on the road an hour ago", I found myself asking out loud.

"What you say Mommy?"

"Just talking to myself. Stay in the car and lock the door. I'll be right back."

His car was parked in the back of the shop. He had to be in there 'cause it wasn't there when I left. Wasn't no lights on, not even the 'Closed' light. Justin wasn't talking loud as usual so he had to be doing something he ain't have no business doing. Them two don't even get along so why in the hell would his car even be here if he hadn't left town yet, knowing that I told him I was on my way home when I talked to him. He said he was on his way to the expressway.

I was about to find out what the hell was going on. I had to take the key off the key ring so it didn't make not one sound when I opened the door. I took my shoes off outside too. I learned to stop being so naive a long time ago dealing with Jeff. I was getting cheated on and lied to about having a job when he didn't, him at home playing some video game while I worked. I had become a regular Inspector Gadget so I knew exactly how to find out what I needed to know.

The first thing I saw was the clothes scattered on the floor. I saw jeans first.

These the fuckin' jeans I just bought his ass, I threw them back down after I verified that size 38. His shirt was on the steps. It had to be that Princess bitch, I thought, creeping through the back corridor, listening for where they could possibly be. I didn't even see Justin. I figured he must've been upstairs in the office 'cause we had at least 30 customers a day. We made a lot of money every day the shop was open. After we locked those doors that money had to be counted and locked up until we got to the bank the next day.

There was no way my brother would know Mike was in the shop without calling me to find out why. Especially around Princess. If anybody knew Princess had hoe tendencies, it was Justin. She was his best friend. Always in the shop late getting all that ghetto weave put in her head every week. Checking my man out when he came up there for me. Ain't no way Jay Jay know he in here and my cell phone didn't ring yet, I looked at the blank screen. It was still in sleep mode.

I wanted to, no I *needed* to, catch them in the act. I was about to beat her ass right there in that shop for disrespecting me, I planned, taking off my gold hoops, slipping them in my back pocket. That bitch knew he was my man. He been coming in here the whole time I been at this damn shop. And watch what happens to *his* ass too.

I was breathing fire by then. They were gonna wish they never met me. Who the hell did they think they were? If it was going to be like this, he could've left me alone and just be with her. Evidently he like that kinda woman. And this MY shop they fucking in! They don't know me, I ranted in my head. And Justin better not say shit, 'cause I feel like he may have something to do with all this, I changed my mind about my dear brother. How *is* he in the shop and don't know what the hell is going on? Where in the hell they at any way?

I had been looking in every room, every closet…that's when I heard the moans. From the bathroom. I didn't think to look in there, I could've kicked myself. What was he doing? Fucking her in the tub?

The door was cracked.

I got down on my knees and peeked around the corner. It *wasn't* her. It *wasn't* Princess.

I couldn't believe it. My legs felt weak. My heart was racing. I just knew I was about to see her bent over the tub with him behind her but it was *him* moaning. I wanted to scream and cuss at him, tell him I wish he was dead but I couldn't do nothing. I went into shock. Was I actually watching my boyfriend, my future husband with another woman? His dick was at full attention. All I could see was her hair at first – and then I saw those big lips: red lipstick – she sucked up his penis in her mouth and it looked as if it disappeared as she licked and caressed one side at a time, both her hands pulling his cheeks in to her.

He was gyrating and his head was laid back. What was going on? Was this shit really happening or was this some sick dream? I could see her claws, cupping his balls and her head began to bob up and down, faster and faster and I heard him then, just as he squirted it all over her face.

"*Damn* Antoine…Damn that felt *good as h-e-l-l*!"

Oh come on! I pleaded. Is there *any*thing else I need to find out GOD? I asked my Savior. Why does this stuff always happen to me? Is this some kind of karma? Antoine was one the damn stylists. If he wasn't one of the best in the city his ass wouldn't have no job! That bitch been listening to me plan my wedding for months all the while you mean to tell me this mothafucka been sucking my man's dick??? How long had they been doing this bullshit?

I crawled to the back door as fast as I could and slipped out. I didn't even bother to close the door all the way. I just ran. I ran so fast I ran right past my brand-new Kate Spade sneakers I was in such a hurry to get to my car. I backed the hell out of that parking lot. I was still seeing him standing there letting another man lick on him and kiss his dick and he was *loving* it. I been with this man for *years*. Too many years to not see this! We *always* had sex, I reasoned with myself. We had a great sex life and he was always turned on. How could he be *gay*?

There was nothing he could possibly say to me. He had to get the fuck out of my house. It was one thing to get cheated on for a woman and a whole*other*fucking thing to catch your man getting his dick sucked by a man who *thought* she was a woman while he knew damn well that she was a 'he'. Antoine. Really Mike? He don't even look *half* as good as I do!

The whole way fucking home I'm thinking about how I need to get an AIDS test somewhere because I hear about all the dudes Antoine got under his belt. I hope he didn't think his dick was the only one in Antoine's mouth! It sure the fuck wasn't! As a matter of fact I should call Marcus and tell him. That'll be exactly what his ass get too if Marcus beat that ass! I couldn't believe that shit. Had the nerve to be dialing my number after what I had just saw. What the fuck was he calling *me* for? He looked pretty satisfied to me. Probably lighting up a cigarette dialing my number.

"Hey *Jacobi*," He called me by my government name. "What you and Kennedy doing?"

He was acting like he gave a fuck.

"Nothin, *WHY*?" I found myself barking at him. "We minding our business at the moment, I see you not minding *yours*."

"Y'all *are* my business lady. I was calling to let you know that I made it to Grandma's and I'll be home in a few days. Maybe Sunday night. If you need something call me, ok?"

Yeah right. I bet he at his grandmother's house. Probably on his way to Antoine's house for round 2. They didn't just start doing this shit. How does that conversation come up? Did he walk up and say 'Come up here and let me suck your dick for you?' or did *Mike* ask for it?

I was disgusted. I was tired of thinking about it. Why was I even on the phone with him for this long? I needed to be planning my next move. He had to get the hell out of my house. And soon. I felt betrayed. By all three of them: him, Toine, and Justin ass. Ain't no way in hell Justin didn't know about it. They talk about who on the down low and who finally gave in. I hear them all the time. I was mad as fuck at all of them for betraying me. Then I started blaming myself. I didn't even see it.

"Yup," I agreed. "I sure will call you if I need something, *Michelle*."

My sarcasm was obvious.

"Michelle?" His voice grew a little. "Who is Mich-?"

I didn't mean to *say* it. I was thinking in my head how much of a *bitch* he was and how I *should* start calling him Michelle

"Boy, I was about to say Michelle, my friend from school, is beeping in but your rude ass interrupted me. I'll call you back."

I didn't even say bye. I just hung up.

Took me all of about a half hour to pack up all his shit. I waited until Kennedy went to sleep and got to packing. I was done with that dude. He was a liar. I sure in the hell wasn't using any of my suitcases to put his clothes in either. All his shit went into 4 Hefty bags. I figured since he was trash that's what he deserved to have his shit put in. I normally hate pop ups, but when Richelle stopped by I was glad to see her. Not only did she have some wine which I definitely needed but somebody could watch over Kennedy just in case I wanted to be irrational.

At first we put all the bags by the back door. I wanted that to be the first thing he saw when he got back. Then it was the porch. He didn't need to come in the house for shit! He wasn't welcome anymore. By the time Good Times went off all 6 of them bags were in the dumpster behind Denny's and I didn't feel bad about hooking back up with Jeff at all. When Florida threw that glass bowl down, the smile I had on my face was me imagining Mike being the one saying 'Damn Damn Damn'!

Chapter 4: Tawana

Every day I was waking up, looking for my cell phone buried under my pillows and sheets to see if I had missed any calls or see if I had any text messages about her. Always paranoid! Here it was 5:00 in the morning and I was scared she may have died while I was sleep. The whole time I was looking for my phone I was hating myself for being tired just in case it did happen and I hadn't even layed eyes on it yet. From the moment my feet hit the floor I felt like I had been up for hours already. Worrying.

The whole time I was getting dressed I was talking to God about my mother. It was gonna happen to all of us one day, but I didn't want that for her. Not yet. I needed him to give me just a little more time with her. She gave the best advice on top of everything else she did and Lord knows that's what I needed. I was literally coming apart at the seams. My life was in shambles! I needed my mother. She was the only sanity I had because mine left a long time ago. Six years ago to be exact. That's when I realized I could talk to her about him because praying wasn't working fast enough. Nothing was working. Talking to her made me feel at least a little better about my situation and about her – her illness. God don't give you nothing you can't handle, but I spent a lot of time pleading with him about Mommy and removing Charles out of my life because I couldn't handle it any longer. I was losing a little more of my mind every single day.

I was depressed and it wasn't getting better. He was fucking with me and I had gotten to the point of everything irritated me. Even the sound of birds chirping would piss me off. He had become some dark cloud in my place and he made sure my days stayed rainy ones. He didn't ask about my mother's health and never wanted to know if I needed anything. It was quite apparent that he flat-out didn't give a damn. Somehow it had become my fault - and he was taking it out on me through his disregard for what I was going through- that he didn't have a family who gave 2 shits about him so he didn't care about mine. I couldn't stop thinking about my family. That 6 months to live they gave Mommy had actually been a death sentence for me every day of the week.

I felt like a zombie towards the end because my life was going to be empty without her. She looked like a skeleton lying there and seeing her bare legs when she took the cover off always took my breath away. They were so scrawny. Who was this lady all sick and weak? Her face was bony and her eyes weren't covered with gold eye shadow and lined with the darkest pencil like they used to be. Their beautiful almond shape was unrecognizable and I didn't see anything familiar in them no matter how hard I tried.

This person was a stranger who reminded me of someone and I needed to get to know her so I could make sense of why she had come to replace my mother. I didn't want to see her like that but I didn't have a choice. I had to be there with her because there was no way in hell I was going to stay away no matter how it made me feel. It wasn't about me when I held her lanky hands. She needed me there to comfort her the same way her and Daddy would comfort me. When I was sick or going through something there was something about my parents being in the same room that made whatever it was easier to deal with. They were my courage. I was on home turf when my parents were around and it wasn't just the strength my Daddy had. It was Mommy's protection. I felt like I could conquer anything with her there. I wanted her to have that now. I could imagine how she felt about what she saw in her mirror. She could see the same thing we saw, those hollow eye sockets and thinning hair.

Dying scared the shit out of me. Daddy looked at the obituaries all the time and he *always* knew somebody. He knew them from church or grew up with them – he used to work with them. It was always somebody in there he knew. When I started paying attention I saw people *I* knew in there. That was what made me start reading them all the time. Pretty soon it was just a part of me reading the newspaper. I think I needed to see the faces of young people like me or anybody I knew in general who had died. It was like facing my fears of dying every time I saw somebody I knew did it. It really hit home when it was somebody I carried on conversations with, you know, was kind of like a friend to. I still wondered how it felt to die. I wanted to know if you could feel when you about to die so I could prepare myself for it. I couldn't bring myself to ask her if she could feel herself dying. What kind of question was that to ask her?

I wasn't used to seeing my mother like that, lying in bed so frail and weak. I remember when she was in the kitchen making coffee or the backyard taking care of her garden. The garden was all weeds the last time I saw it. She spent hours on her knees picking weeds and putting down fresh dirt for new flowers. Who was going to do that now? Just a garden full of weeds just like Mommy can't look like a million dollars anymore. She was the shell of who she used to be. The hardest thing I ever had to do was to watch her wither away, knowing she was at the end of her life.

She knew if I could've quit my job I would have. I even told her that, but she said she didn't mind Cathy taking care of her. I wouldn't have minded either if Cathy was a different type of person. I never agreed with Daddy about her being the aide. Especially living in the house. She wouldn't have gotten hired as an aide in the real world so why was she good enough to move in and take care of my mother? Because she went to the same church? That didn't mean shit. What about being able to take care of somebody? Obviously she wasn't good at that because she didn't take care of all the kids she gave birth to. You can't just have a bunch of kids and pick a few of them to keep like puppies. Yet this is the type of person you picked to be in the house with my dying mother because she said she was a *Christian*?

The whole reason why she was there in the beginning was because she needed an address for when she got out. Since she couldn't go no where on that monitor Daddy decided she could take care of Mommy? Daddy said her PO could monitor her at the house. Plus he said they were friends and used to sing in the choir together. That was what made the bitch a good choice? That didn't make it a

good choice in my opinion. I'm sure if we could have sat down –
all of us – we could have come up with a better plan instead of
getting involved with Cathy and all her drama. I get mad every time
I think about it to this day.

Cathy was the one who told me Mommy wouldn't be here for too
much longer. I couldn't hear everything she was saying because she
was talking so low in the phone. I knew she was gossiping about
something because that's what she does. Always gotta be the first
one to tell somebody else's business. The old bitty couldn't hold
water so she couldn't wait to pick up the phone when they left the
doctor's office. I guess it didn't matter to her how that was going to
make me feel in the middle of my shift. All she cared about was
being the first to break the news which wasn't her place to do. In a
way I thought her reason for doing it was because she knew how
much I didn't like her. That was probably her way of getting me
back for what I always said about her.

Mommy didn't want us to know. She knew it would kill us to hear
something like that. I would have rathered she didn't tell me like
Mommy told her not to do. It wasn't like we couldn't see she was
dying! We just didn't know how long she had to live, 6 months or
2 weeks. If I had a choice, which Cathy didn't give me, I wouldn't
have wanted to know. Especially finding out over the phone at my
damn job! I didn't know if I more pissed off that she told me on the
phone or that she told me on the phone when I was at work. I
couldn't believe the old bitch had the nerve to upset me like that at
my job. After I heard it I just hung the phone up. What the fuck did
she think I was going to say? I just left. I cried all the way to
Mommy's house and didn't say shit to her when I got there. Thank
you my ass! Why would I need to tell you 'thank you' because you
told me my mother was going to die in 6 months?

I was lost whenever I saw Cathy's number. I couldn't even answer
it. I would literally crawl up in a ball in the corner and just cry. I
didn't want to hear anything she was calling to tell me. I knew that
one of her phone calls eventually was going to be her calling to tell
me that my life had just ended. My life was going to be over too the

moment Mommy died. I had started thinking about how I could take my life so I never had to hear it.

Daddy had always told us suicide would be a one-way ticket to Hell, but it didn't matter to me about Heaven or Hell. Hell was where I would be any way if I had to live without her. I thought I would be able to handle it when the time came, but I couldn't. It was affecting every move I made. Even my thought process was off. I wasn't Tawana no more. Tawana rationalized every little thing she did. I didn't know how to rationalize during that time.

It got to the point where I couldn't explain why I was acting out because I learned the process of death and dying. I saw it all the time. I saw people die from diseases and the doctors couldn't save them. We saw drug overdoses and when they made it to us it was already too late to bring them back with Narcan. People died all the time. But I guess I found out how different it was. I didn't know those people. I didn't love them. Mommy dying wasn't the same. She had breast cancer, not some drug addict addicted to drugs. Narcan would never be able to cure what she had.

Time went too quick. Just like that there we were. I knew chemotherapy wasn't going to save her life but it offered some kind of false hope. Maybe it didn't have to be inevitable that she was going to die. The doctors didn't always know the life expectancy of another person. Wasn't that God's job? She could live 5 or 10 more years if the chemo worked on her. How did they know about *my* mother's will to live? She could fight anything just the same as she had done all of my life! She could do that now too I prayed. God knew how taking her away would destroy me. I was his child too so he knew me just like he knew her. Maybe he would change his mind about taking her from this earth in the final hour. For my own selfish reasons I didn't want her to stop going to her treatments. How could I take the chance of not knowing if it would help her in the end?

I needed my mom like I did when I was a 5-year-old girl. Not just to help me with the regular stuff you need your mom for like recipes or how to grow plants. She had to help keep me sane! This life stuff wasn't for me. When Lamille gave me that shit – that PCP – I didn't even pay no attention to what she said it was. We had only taken OxyContin and Vicodin, I didn't think I had to ask what she was giving me. I never thought she would give me street drugs knowing I had never in my life taken anything like that at that time. I would have settled for Tylenol 3 at least. I trusted her judgment like an idiot.

I was hanging on by a piece of thread. Drinking. As much as I hated the drunk I was married to I was drinking shots of vodka before work to help me get through shifts. I had to intoxicate myself to be around my patients because the smell of disease made me ill. If that hospital had of found out I was giving injections and passing out medication damn near drunk they would have had me arrested. I wouldn't be a nurse anymore that's for sure. The fact that Mommy was on the board at the hospital wouldn't be able to save me if I tested positive on any of those random drug tests they did. I had been lucky. At least with one thing in my life.

Chapter 5: Tawana's Dream

When we got together we liked the same foods and watched the same shows on TV. We could have even been mistaken for a couple in love in the very beginning. That was the quickest 2 weeks I have ever seen! Too bad those days were long gone. It was all about who could win the argument and destroy the other one. He had made me a vindictive bitch and I was all about paying him back for whatever he put me through even if it was subtle things. He never put his hands on me, but his words were fighting words. I felt it was my duty to make him pay for every disrespectful word that came out of his drunk-ass mouth. Who the hell did he think he was? I found myself dumping out his heart medication and dropping his toothbrush in the toilet, hoping it would dry before he realized it was already wet. A few times I called that hotline to report a drunk driver. He didn't know who he was dealing with!

Even with all that, it still failed. He never got pulled over and he was still alive. It was no use. I wanted him to leave and he wanted to stay just to make me miserable. On top of being worried about my mom I was worried about which one of his drunken demons he would bring home after work to torment me. Was it going to be Happy, Sloppy, or Violent Demon? My reality was that my mother was dying and I had managed to marry an alcoholic who would probably end up just like the ones I saw every day at the hospital. Who would have known when I started working there that I could end up being that wife sitting next to the bed of an alcoholic husband dying of cirrhosis of his liver?

The part that pissed me off was that he never wanted to admit he had a problem. Always said he was fine. Never could remember anything that happened, but was always 'fine', stumbling over furniture that hadn't been moved and talking like he had a whole mouth full of nasty spit. Who knows…maybe it wasn't just alcohol that had him under the influence. Either way I used to pray to God he would pack his stuff and go live somewhere else. We couldn't stand each other. We didn't get along and he wasn't interested in changing it. The man couldn't get it through his head that it would be better for both of us if he would just leave. Needless to say *THAT* never happened. For years he went out and got drunk and no matter how much I prayed, he always made it right back home like a damn wicked boomerang as if I threw his ass out there.

It was a shame how whatever he poured down his throat governed how my night was going to end. It was never a good day for me. I can't point out a single good day in years. Yeah we got along sometimes, but not a whole day. Charles was what you would call a 'petty' man. His feminine ways were the cause of a lot of our disagreements. Women like to argue is what they say and that was true about him, that feminine side of him. He had to have all the answers even when his dumb ass couldn't comprehend the questions. When I explained my questions it was the insult that started the whole thing in his opinion. In that fucked up brain of his, spelling it out was the same as calling him stupid. Those were the sober times.

Daddy didn't like it, but I didn't want to go to no church. Why should I go to the house of the Lord and pray when he wasn't interested in the prayers that came from my house? Was it going to change what I was asking for if I did it from the church? Whose side was God on anyway? He certainly wasn't on my side because look at what I was dealing with. One of his children needed an exorcism and he didn't seem too interested in helping him. I didn't see the point of going to church on Sunday just to be miserable again on Sunday night. Then again on Monday, Tuesday, Wednesday. I asked God for two things. Two things only. I didn't see any improvement. I even told Daddy I wanted to kill him. You know what he said? That God defines murder as any feelings of deep-seated hatred or malice against him. If that was the truth then he was already dead so why was I going through this? Why couldn't I just blow his brains out?

It was all about survival and death. The only 2 words I knew. Did Mommy pass away and I wish he were dead and how can I survive one more day of all this bullshit were the questions I had for as far back as I could remember before I went crazy. There was nothing I could do about Mommy's situation, but if God could at LEAST remove one problem I may not kill myself after all. There were days I waited for the news to see if there had been a fatal accident happening in Georgia somewhere. Danny Dinehart would say it was a 2014 Chevrolet Impala that crashed into some pole and I would get out the wine glasses. That was how I dealt with it.

I daydreamed about how my days would be if something happened to him. Cruel, maybe, but to me it was going to be the end of a prison sentence just that it wasn't in a prison. How would I change my house around and what type of wardrobe was I gonna buy for myself as a single woman when he was gone? Yeah it was sad that I had to think that way, but wasn't that the reality of dealing with an alcoholic? It was for me. Wishing something would happen to him while he was drunk didn't make me responsible for it if it did happen. He was his own worse enemy first and I was next.

That stupid time clock freed him at 4:00. Beelzebub had to drink every day of the week so by 4:15 the first beer was gone. I never knew when it would happen, but some of those days it was the shots of cheap liquor. On those days by 4:30 I was despising the fact that alcohol existed. *A half hour*. That was all the time it took for him to morph into one of his characters.

The countdown was on for me after 4. Damn. I only had 2 ½ hours of sanity before I would have to pull on my suit of armor to defend myself against whatever demon he was turning into.

I never did find out why I was always the target. The very first time it happened I was actually in shock. Here I was thinking I had found my knight in shining armor agreeing to marry him and his main focus wasn't even me. Not me as a person. I was self-sufficient and he knew that. He was probably thinking if we got together he wouldn't have any responsibilities and it would be on me to take care of everything. His check could be all his if I took care of everything. His priority wasn't taking care of me or the house. It was the bottle. Or a can. A can of Milwaukee's Best Ice. Hunh! That was the BEST ice? I didn't think it was.

He was outright belligerent depending on what he had. I never had a problem trying to help him with anything and he would always say that he didn't know what he would do without me. I was the best he had ever had, he reminded me whenever he was sober, but in that other state of mind, I was his one and only enemy, being called every name except the one given to me at birth. I learned to stay prepared dealing with him. I promised myself that was never going to happen again, him having the upper hand. I found out that deep inside he enjoyed ripping off my head and trying to shit down my neck to take the weight of the world off of his shoulders.

There I was trying to keep my sanity for 12 hours taking care of other sick people and not being able to take care of my own sick mother. I was dealing with Charles's bullshit at the same time. It was too much! I would manage to hold in tears for my whole shift at work just to come home and be in my own personal hell with Charles. I worried about how my night would end up until I had made myself sick with the anticipation of it. My legs were wet noodles by then, not wanting to go home even after working all those hours away from it. Listening to the dozen voice messages he would leave about me not being shit and taking bets with myself about the number of insults he could fit into each message.

Some dude Lamille had just met gave her pills. He didn't tell her what they could do he just gave them to her. She told me he wanted to sleep with her and she didn't want to so she kept telling him she had too much on her mind to start a new relationship. That was the excuse she gave him so he supposedly gave those to her so they could 'take her mind off' of them for a little while. It never dawned on her that he didn't ask her for nothing for them. Ain't no body giving away pills like that. Pills like that sell for enough to buy a pack of cigarettes or a full tank of gas. People don't give pills away for free. Unless they have another motive. That should have been the first red flag.

Lamille feels like she can trust any and everybody. She is way too trusting. I tell her all the time she can't take people's pills and smoke weed with just anybody. Everybody ain't your friend. You might be smoking crack and not even know. Sitting there thinking you just smoking some weed with Timmy because y'all live in the same apartment building and next thing you know you're hooked and can't get off of it. She don't think about stuff that way. It finally scared her because she sure didn't take those pills.

Good thing she didn't take them. I could have lost my best friend that night. He could have been a killer for all she knew. His plans could have been to drug, rape, and kill her. She didn't know him like that. She met him in some hole-in-a-wall bar and had no idea what he could be capable of. I'm glad she finally started thinking about what I told her because she held onto them. When he got up to go to the bathroom she put the damn pills in her wallet instead of throwing them in the garbage. I don't know why she didn't just throw them away. That's how I ended up with them. Lamille had no idea that when she left those pills on my table my life as I knew it was about to end.

It was her fault I went crazy like that. I wanted to blame her. For all of it. She was the one who did dumb shit to the extreme not me. *I* was her rational friend. It was me always telling her what I thought was a bad idea not the other way around. If it wasn't for me that girl with the heart full of good intentions would've donated half of her child support check to the kids in Africa instead of her own. It ain't been too long ago that she planned on surprising me with 6 bottles of Miracle Spring Water to bring my spirits up. Knowing what kind of person she was there was no way I could put me taking them pills on her even if I wanted to. I knew better than to just take some strange medicine that wasn't my own prescription. That was something that had been pounded into my head from the day I started nursing school. I wasn't thinking that night. Mommy used to fuss at me for saying that. She used to say, 'You should *never* tell *no* body you weren't thinking!' I wasn't though.

It was a Monday. I had never had a day like that. It was a madhouse! I had 7 patients on Medsurg and we were understaffed because I didn't have a CNA. Janet called off. I couldn't believe she did that. Without her, I had to do vitals and blood sugars. There was no one else to help me turn my people every 2 hours and answer call lights. I was doing it all. I couldn't get through a complete assessment without a call light ringing for the bathroom or water. 'I need my medicine!', or 'Nurse!' was all I heard the whole shift. I could hear the call lights in my head on my lunch break.

There was no way I was going to make it through the whole shift without going crazy. The text messages had already started. Violent drunk was coming home that night. Damn! I really wanted to blow my brains out at that point. That was when I texted Lamille. He wasn't getting a rise out of me that night. I needed something that was going to knock me out, I told her, because I didn't even have so much as an Advil tablet.

It drove his insecurities about himself to upset me and I knew he would be looking forward to picking with me as soon as he came through the door. That's what he did every time. If I was watching T.V. in the living room he was drawn to it…standing in front of the screen…mad if I dared ask him to move. I think it was all because he knew he wasn't worth my time. The only way he could get any attention from me was to control my anger. Somehow that man knew what liquors he should concentrate on and the number of Milwaukee's Best Ice he should drink so he could add the perfect amount of salt to the wounds of my worse days. I believe he lived to be able to do that.

Violent Drunk was the most intimidating out of all of them, curling his lips into a snarl every time he called me a 'bitch', prepared to ball his fist if I dared respond with 'bitch' back to him. He always had the nerve to tell me, 'Don't disrespect me', when I defended myself. Just the thought of the impending standoff had my nostrils flaring and I couldn't let him win. I was taking a different route. Maybe he couldn't argue if I didn't say anything, like my mother said. I was going to find out. By the time the bars closed I would be locked away in that bedroom and he was going to be the last thing on my mind.

I couldn't get comfortable. I was tossing and turning back and forth! My whole body was shaking because my heart was beating so fast. I was sweating bullets. I was in my bed wearing nothing but a pair of panties because I was so hot I had to take off my gown. I was always cold in that room so something was wrong with me. My room was never hot. It was *always* cold. I usually kept the space heater on in there just to keep it kinda warm otherwise I would freeze to death. Why was it so hot all of a sudden? I had no idea what was going on. What the fuck did those pills do to me? It felt like I couldn't breathe. It was all stuffy. Almost like the walls were closing in on me.

I closed my eyes hoping it would all go away. Please don't let this be real I begged God. I know I had been mad at him and stopped praying as much, but please help me God! I can't fix this! No one can fix it but you Lord! That's when I started hearing the voices.

I didn't know where they were coming from at first. The only light I had was the one from the streetlight outside the window. I couldn't see anybody. I could just hear voices. I couldn't understand what they were saying but whatever it was they were talking fast. It didn't sound like they were speaking English. That shit had me hallucinating. It was weird. I had never hallucinated before but I had to be because it seemed like a dream but I wasn't sleep. What was happening to me?

I kept rubbing my eyes, trying to make it all normal again and it wasn't working. I was having a real nightmare I figured. My nightmare had started off like the beginning of a horror film and I didn't want to go through the whole thing. I pinched myself so hard

I took the skin off my arm. It wasn't some nightmare because I wasn't sleep!

After that I could see 3 shadows on my wall and their voices were loud and clear. I don't know how they knew me but they had found me after all that time they were saying. Then I heard them say they were going to kill me. They knew my name. I heard them with my own ears. Kill Tawana?

Kill me? I didn't even know those people! Why would they have a reason to want *me* dead? I had never done anything to anybody! If it was something they wanted from my house why couldn't they just take it and leave me alone? That was another reason why I hated Charles. What kind of husband was he? Instead of him being home to protect me he was drunk off his ass somewhere. He was out playing house with one of his girlfriends while I was about to be another statistic.

I was so scared all I could do was get off that floor and try to get out of there as fast as I could. I was moving in slow motion. I was going to die! I never looked back. I was screaming and praying to GOD the whole time that my neighbor would see something was wrong with that window being open. She was nosy so she spent all her time watching everybody's house. If she was up I know she would see what was going on and call 9-1-1! My window was never open. That would make her suspicious right away. Why would my window be wide open at this time of night of something weren't going on like this? A home invasion. Charles's car wasn't in the driveway. That meant I was the only one at home and I must be in trouble. There's no way I would have my window wide open in the middle of the night and there were no screens in them. I had a Chihuahua for Heaven's sake not a pit bull. Maybelline wasn't a threat! She was *still* hiding under the bed when I ran out of there!

I was hallucinating something awful! I was under the table sweating like I had run a marathon and I could not stop shaking. I needed water. I needed to drink some water and pour it all over my body at the same time. I was dehydrated I think. If I didn't think those men would jump out at any time I think I would have taken the chance to crawl to the bathroom. There was a lock on the door. At least I could hide in there and drink from the faucet. I was about to pass out and they would be able to take me and do whatever they came there to do to me. I didn't know what I was going to do. All I could think about was dying and not being able to see my Mommy for the last time. I didn't want to die like that. This couldn't be my fate. I just refused to accept that.

That's when Charles came stumbling in the back door. I didn't hear him pull up. Oh my GOD! He had no idea what was going on. I needed to warn him. I was whispering as loud as I could. I couldn't get any louder than that without them knowing where I was.

"Charles…over here! I'm in the dining room! There's people in here! Charles! We gotta get out of here!" I was trying to tell him. "They want to kill me!"

It was like he couldn't hear me. He walked right past the dining room and was standing there – in the living room. I don't know when they did it, but his clothes and shoes were piled up in the middle of the living room floor. I didn't smell it before, but I could smell bleach. It was strong. One of them must've poured the whole bottle all over it, because he was standing there cussing and picking up different shirts and shoes, holding the shit up so he could see what was wrong with it. Why couldn't he hear me? I couldn't get any louder than I was. Then they would know where I was hiding.

As much as I hated him I was glad he was there so the least I could do was warn his drunk ass. For once in our entire marriage I was glad he came in that door so I wasn't by myself. I didn't care about him being drunk. At least the two of us would have a better chance at getting them out of there than I would have by myself. Charles usually carried his gun Maybe he had it on him. If he had it on him then we were going to be okay because the knives they had wouldn't be a match for a gun, right? I needed to tell him because he didn't know what was going on. He still couldn't hear me.

Right when I was about to crawl from under the table I saw them. Not their actual bodies, I could see their shadows. They were surrounding him and he didn't look scared. He was telling them something because I could see his lips moving. They were reading his lips.

He knew they were there the whole time! He was ignoring me! He was the one who put them up to it, to scare me. That's how they got in my house. Charles left the window open for them. He told them to scare me. Or kill me. He's the one trying to get rid of me. It all made sense at that point.

If I was out of the picture him and one of his girlfriends could live happily ever after in my house. That would never happen! He didn't spend one dime in that house. He didn't help me pay bills there. No electric bill, gas bill, or water bill. He didn't sell those drugs to help me take care of my house! I wasn't just going to lay there and let them *kill* me so he could have the house *I* paid for. I was done hiding. It was all out in the open. He was in on it.

"You were behind all of this?" I wanted to know. "You put them up to this? Breaking in here to kill me?"

"Awww bitch you is crazy! What's wrong with you?"

He had the nerve to act like I was imagining it. I was tripping at first but I understand exactly what was going on when I saw how he was acting when he came in. He wasn't surprised. This was all his doing. I had figured out how I had gotten to where I was. It was Charles. He was behind all of it.

He was arguing with me like I made it all up. I wasn't crazy and he knew it! Once again he was blaming me for something he was responsible for. I had never taken anything like that and he knew what it would do to me. Somehow he figured out a way to drug me so he could get rid of me. He had it all set up. If I were to get killed he could have everything – my house, my money. There's no way he didn't think about killing me as much as I wished he would drop dead. Every nook and cranny was always preoccupied with his last breath so I'm sure that feeling was mutual. He thought he had found a way to get rid of me and look at me. I foiled it.

Maybe it was him and Lamille. I don't care if she didn't like him or not. He was still her brother. Blood is thicker than water no matter what. She didn't have a lot of money. Maybe he promised her some money from my life insurance policy after they killed me. Anything is possible.

He was in the refrigerator asking me a bunch of questions with his damn back to me like I was so beneath him. He couldn't even look at me! Was he expecting me to answer any of his fucking questions and he wasn't even looking at me in my face? It had to be a trick. He was trying to play it off. He knew what was going on! The monsters were blocking me in and I had nowhere to go even if I wanted to get out of there. I had my knife so they were more than welcome to try it! I was going to try to get as many of them as I could and Charles would be the first one I would get. He had to pay for all the times he jumped up in my face. I hated him for disrespecting me every time he came in drunk and targeted me like I had done him so wrong. I wasn't the problem. He was the goddamn one with the problem. Hell HE was *my* problem. Stayed so drunk he couldn't understand it was all his fault we were in the bad place we were in.

He was going to pay for all the pain he had caused me that night. I don't remember seeing the monsters after that. I only remember him in the kitchen. I wasn't afraid anymore. I felt strong. My heart wasn't racing like it did whenever we got into it. I wanted him to try to bully me like he usually did. I would always stand my ground with him even though I knew I wouldn't win. I was always ready to fight as hard as I could. Tonight I wanted it to end different from it always had before. I wanted him to try it while the magic pills were in control. He wasn't fighting with Tawana. I may as well been those devils myself.

"You dirty bitch. You ain't no wife to me. I should whoop your ass."

"I'm not playing with you Charles. You HEAR me? I will kill you! I HATE you!"

"Girl you crazy! You all talk. You ain't gone do shit. You cheating on me BITCH! Your boyfriend gave you some bad shit hunh?"

That's when he grabbed me around my neck and pinned me against the damn wall. All I could see in my head was that part in this movie when that man grabbed his wife around her neck every time he felt like she said the wrong thing. Whenever she tried to confront him about what he was doing wrong or had an opinion he didn't think she should have the first thing he did was reach out and grab her around her neck. Through the whole movie. Finally at the end when he tried to kill her, he grabbed her around the neck, but that time she fucked him up. He wasn't expecting that. She had secretly took self defense classes because she wanted to divorce him and knew he would try to kill her. She wanted to learn how to protect herself. She learned kickboxing and how to get out of different holds. She turned into Jackie Chan. I watched that movie so much I knew how to do it too. I imagined it being me fighting like that. I could see myself beating the hell out of Charles. I did it. That's exactly what I did to him.

When he grabbed me I lifted my arm straight up in the air and brought it down across both his arms. I turned and back kicked his ass as hard as I could. When he went down I remember jumping on top of him and stabbing him. I just kept stabbing and stabbing until he wasn't moving. He couldn't hurt me any more. I didn't have to listen to his insults and his belittling me. I was done smelling the rotten stench on his breath calling me name after name. I never had to hear it again. I killed him. He was dead. Charles was laying there dead so I had to bury him so I wouldn't get caught. I crawled outside so no body could see me and dug a hole as fast as I could. That's how my dream ended.

My head hurt so bad when I woke up I couldn't even sit up on the side of the bed. Just moving to my side disturbed all the blood vessels in my head. Any little movement, even breathing constricted my blood vessels. That blood pushing though those narrow vessels was killing me! I was convinced it was going to be the death of me. My temples were throbbing like there was a man with a hammer in there banging to escape. My mouth was dry. I could have sworn I swallowed a whole bale of hay in my sleep. I needed something to drink – a tall glass of water - but there was no way in hell I was about to move.

I was just laying there trying to figure out how I got to my Daddy's house. I had been laying there for a while thinking about that damn nightmare I had over and over in my head. My fingers were tight. They were burning and hurt like hell. I couldn't wait to tell Lamille what she had done to me by handing me those pills. I was trying to figure out how I was going to roll out of bed to turn on the light. I needed to actually see why my fingers were on fire and at least look in the mirror. I needed to find out if my head was enlarged or something to be throbbing the way it was. It kept replaying in my head over and over.

Something bad had happened. I must've been so scared I drove to Daddy's in the middle of the night. Yeah that had to be it. He beat me up this time, but I can't remember because of those pills. They had me hallucinating and having nightmares. That was a hell of a nightmare. I was fighting for my life in that dream. What I'm thinking happened is that he came in drunk and hit me because why else would I be at Daddy's? I was so out of it, I'm thinking all I could do to protect myself was grab my keys and drive to Daddy's house. He would protect me from Charles just like him and Mommy always did. That had to be why I was there. Even in the state of mind I was in that's something I would've done - get to my daddy to save me.

I needed to get up and at least look at my hands. I needed to go to the ER the way they felt. If I can just turn on the light I can at least look at my hands. He wasn't getting away with it! I told him if he ever put his hands on me I was going to kill him.

When I flipped that light switch all I had on was a robe and my Isotoner slippers on my feet. My feet were swollen. I was covered in blood. I had blood on my face, my hands. My fingers were cut up. That wasn't no damn nightmare. Oh my GOD! What the fuck did I do??? Did that really happen? If I had blood all over my body and my fingers were cut up something did happen at my house. I didn't dream that shit. I had to have stabbed him. I must've killed him! In that dream I buried him. Oh God!!! What am I gonna do???!!!

Chapter 6: Larry

"Did you confess Mr. Lancaster?"

"Yeah. Eventually."

"Didn't you ask for an attorney before they started asking questions? They have to read your Miranda rights Mr. Lancaster. Do you remember hearing that? That's when they let you know 'You have the right to remain silent, anything you say can and will be...' "

"Yeah they said all that, man, but what was I supposed to say when they came to my door? Man at that point when they knockin' on the door at 6 o'clock in the morning it's obvious they got a real strong suspicion. Fuzz knew the deal before they got there what I did. Cassie is my...I love Cassie. She my little girl Mr. Battle. I did what any father would do. I got me a chance to protect my daughter sir. I took that. I did it. Ain't no two ways about it. I did it."

"I have read everything on this case. I'm the attorney who is going to represent you. I am going to do everything I can to help you given the fact that you freely gave a confession without my being present. It could be a case of coercion, duress. They can't assume that because you have a criminal record you would likely be the suspect in Todd's homicide."

"I don't know what you want me to say. Ain't no way out of this. Like the man told me, my daughter had it posted all over Facebook what her boyfriend did to her, how he humiliated her. He was gay Attorney Battle. He embarrassed my daughter. And what about my grandbaby? That baby living her life around a daddy that's some punk. I ain't want that for her. He was on my shit list when she brought him over there to meet us in the first place. I prayed then he didn't do nothin' sideways to land me back in prison."

"I would like to start from the top. I want to hear the story directly from you. Every detail. Please."

"You know how you hear them stories? Them stories that you don't be thinkin' is too real. About people going missin' and when they get found all they organs gone? That shit always did have me wonderin' if that shit was true. Sound like it's some bullshit if you ask me. How you pull something like that off? You can kidnap a man and take his organs out, hunh? And then get paid for the organs. I ain't wanna think that way. That would be everybody's answer if you can set your enemies up and use they organs to make some money. Everybody would be doing it and that's what's so scary about it. I got a few enemies I don't care nothin' about. Guess who was on that list?"

"Todd?"

"Most definitely. Most definitely. I hated that little thug mothafucka. With a passion. It was always somethin' about that cat that I couldn't stand. He tried too damn hard. He wanted to try to impress us. He automatically came across like he was hidin' somethin'. I told Cassie – I told that girl – I don't like that young cat Cassie. Cassandra, look, girl, I know what type of dude he is. He come across as trying to be too much of a thug. I encouraged her to go meet up with one of the smart dudes in her class. Anybody except him. Somebody college bound. Not him. He didn't want shit out of life."

"And what did she say when you suggested she date another boy?"

"She wasn't trying to hear me you know what I mean? She young at that time. Anything her mama and daddy want is the opposite of what she wants. That's just how that is. I didn't want nothing bad to happen to her. She my heart. I didn't get a chance to be around my son. I know you read it there, but there was an accident that went down when he was 5…his mother was charging at me and I was already mad, old as I was fighting with some muscle-headed cat and I – well I hit her and she ended up falling and hit her head. It killed her. I didn't mean for none of that to happen. Manslaughter. Missed a lot of his life. He smart too. In college when I got out. Held me at a distance for a long time behind that."

"What happened Mr. Lancaster? What happened that caused you to take the course of action you did?"

"I was in love with Theresa. Theresa was my life. From the time I seen her she was my world, you know? She wasn't stuck up nothing like that, but she wanted what she wanted. She loved me but I was stuck in my ways. We was different. I had an old car, she liked new cars. She lived out in a pretty decent area but my house was in the inner city. She had to make sure her doors was locked when she came to my house. It was paid for but that area wasn't so good. Man she was able to convince me to get a new car and we bought this big house way out in the suburbs. How was I paying for all that? A whole lot of overtime at work. She divorced me."

"Divorced you? Did I miss something?"

"Naw, you didn't miss it. Hard to believe, hunh? Yeah. My wife wanted a divorce because I was always at work. Man she told me we didn't get to spend too much time together so she was done with me. Like I said man – my bad, attorney – like I told you before. My car was old but it was mine. I didn't owe no body for it. I didn't have no car payment, no car note nothing like that. And that house I had I paid that off. I got it and fixed that up. Only paid $12,000. I got it for nothing but the taxes owed on it. Sheriff's sale."

"She had a problem with that, your ex-wife? That freed up a lot of money. New couple, practically no big bills to pay like rent or car payment on your part."

"She wasn't interested in living there. It was all about her. She was my new wife. I was cool with doing whatever I needed to do to make her happy. That was what broke us up. Trying to make her happy. Crazy as hell ain't it? Come to find out after all that took place, my man Mitch told me when I was sitting up in jail that she was talking to her cousin about buying that house we bought out there. The surprise to that was she wanted me back."

"What exactly did Mitch tell you? At what point was she planning on remarrying you? And how did he know what her plan was?"

"Mitch…Elaine's ex-husband. He was Theresa's brother-in-law. He used to come see me up in the joint. Brought my son to see me whenever he was up to it. Elaine took custody of my son. Her and Mitch – they was cool after they went their own separate ways. Jay was there with Elaine and Mitch's daughter Tawana. Ironically, attorney, Mitch got his calling. He wasn't the same ole' cat he used to be. A preacher. He got his calling to be a preacher. He started helping other cats that was like how he was in the beginning. He was talking to all of them. Ended up setting up a prison ministry."

"And that's how you were able to see him? Mitch would bring Jason or you call him - Jay right?"

"Yeah. Yup. Lil Jay. I try to catch myself with that. His brother or really his cousin for real, he go by that name Jay. He a little fruity so he can have the name. My son name Jason. But yeah, it surprised me to see Mitch. He was surprised to see me too. He didn't know where I ended up. I had joined the little bible study group. I got religious in there. Me along with a whole lot of other cats up in there by accident like I was. You know everybody didn't do what they was convicted of in the joint. Here I was another one of 'em. Not guilty. Steve signed up for Mitch's group. He was in my cell. I figured 'why not?' I went on down there with him. And there Mitch is. In a suit. I had never in my life seen that cat in no suit."

"Was he angry at you for what happened to his sister-in-law?"

"I don't think he was angry per se. Like I said, we was brother-in-laws. We got married before they did I thought but that wasn't even the case. Man them two had snuck and got married and didn't tell no body."

"Why did they do that?"

"Probably 'cause he wasn't doing nothing good back then. And both of them was young. Her parents weren't agreeing to nothing like that. They had snuck and got married before we did though."

"So you and Mitch had history with each other then. I can understand that."

"We was in the same family. Married to sisters. Mitch knew my character. I wasn't no violent dude. Pretty sure he knew it had to be an accident. He never asked me."

"When you got out of prison how did you feel? Did you want to reconnect with your past?"

"I didn't have to reconnect with none of them. Elaine and Mitch was the ones who came and picked me up. I stayed in touch. They was my family. All I had was my mama. I didn't know who my real family was. My mama was the lady who adopted me when I was a little baby. I was the only child she had."

"That is good news. At least your son had his aunt and uncle. Glad to hear they got back together. You said they had a separation during the time Elaine had your son?"

"Oh, naw naw. They got divorced. It's a lot of story behind that one. Let's just say that since they was so young when they were together they found out they could be better friends as grown people."

"Ok. But they both had a hand in raising Jason?"

"Yeah. For sure. They both my family. We all one big family. They know I would've never wanted nothing to happen to my wife."

"You still call Theresa your 'wife'? What does Karen think about that?"

"Man she would kill me if she knew I said that. I'm sure she know deep inside that I still love Theresa. It was never over as far as I was concerned."

"And what about the divorce? You signed the papers. You agreed to the divorce."

"I know I did. But all that didn't mean nothing to me. I was gone keep trying to get her back. If she was alive today we would be together. I was willing to do anything to win her back. Anything. I was gonna die trying."

"When did you meet Karen?"

"I met Karen after I got out the joint. The only place I could find that would hire a convict. She was the secretary over there. Packaging place."

"Did she know? I mean about the conviction."

"Yeah she did. I didn't hide nothing. I put it down on my application. Being the secretary I know she saw it. Before I told her about it. Hey man, I didn't do nothing intentionally. Wasn't no sense hiding what went down. It's all public record."

"I am not saying that you tried to hide the facts from your wife Mr. Lancaster. I was wondering if she knew why you went to prison. That it was because of Theresa's death."

"I told her all that. Yeah. First thang."

"So then Cassie was born and you go on and life was good. She grows up and meets the bad guy. Take me to that time in your life."

"He wasn't no real man. Runnin' the street all hours of the night. I done seen shit like that before. We all knew what he was doin'. Cass knew it. She was upset all the time. I just kept getting more and more pissed. I didn't like seeing my baby girl like that."

"When did you first meet him? Did he go to her school?"

"Neighborhood boy. Todd was older than Cassie. Had about 5 years on her. That was my other problem with him."

"Did you try to talk to the guy? Let him know that you did not approve of the way he was handling your daughter?"

"I tried talking to him. Karen talked to him…he didn't give a damn. After I found out he was messing around with Elaine's son – I just…I snapped."

"He was messing with her *son*? So Cassie's boyfriend was bisexual. Of course you weren't happy about that. I know that it was on social media and a lot of people were confused by that information."

"Yeah they was confused. Who wouldn't have been confused? I knew it was something about him like I had figured. Supposed to been one of the biggest gang bangers. I knew it. I knew something was off with him. One night we was sitting up there talking about that. The organs. It sounded good. We read this story about it and next thang you know we was on YouTube. Reading about how people done came up missing like that."

"Go on."

"A lot of people. All kinds of conspiracy theories and look like some real people it happened to. We was laying up there looking at actual news stories, going from story to story looking at missing people. Reading about how they found the bodies with they organs gone."

"Did you believe it?"

"I believed it. I believed it after I got off YouTube and searched the names on Google. They was real people. I even saw the news stories about them. Karen didn't believe it. She said it was fake."

"What made you so interested in something like that?"

"Todd."

"I would like a full understanding of the events that took place…at the time of your – *interest in* those that are missing – was Todd in fact living at the residence with Cassandra?"

"Yeah. He was livin' wit her. Her and Kara. My grandbaby. He was there causing all them problems. Making my little girl miserable is what he was there doing. I was at my wit's end with that dude Attorney. To be honest with you I wanted him gone. I wanted him out of there."

"The agents were able to take the history from your computer. The search warrant did allow them to search your residence and at that time the computer was taken to the station and searched thoroughly."

"I ain't denying *none* of it. How can I deny that? I already done told you I was lookin' up missing people and reading all that shit about them bodies. They was disappearing in the desert and shit. That's some strange shit Attorney. 'Specially how when the bodies turn up ain't no eyes, heart, liver…major organs. One story I was reading the police didn't even find that shit out the extraordinary. I wanted to know if it was a black market for that kind of stuff."

"I have here a copy of what they were able to find out. They saw that search. See here? Item #33: How to find the black market. The other searches are here too, like this one: What is the Black Market…Organs bought on the black market…"

"Yeah of course that's on there. I don't know shit about that. Ain't never heard of no Black Market so I looked it up. You know anything about it? Before you took my case?"

"I heard of cases. A few of them was right here in Georgia and I agree. Very unusual. I must admit I wasn't close to any of those investigations. To be very frank, Mr. Lancaster and that does happen to be my name - I didn't want to know about them. I am a bit old-fashioned. I choose to maintain my old-style ideas. That was simply not heard of when I was coming up. Kidnappings happened but were rare, we could keep doors unlocked. You know. Same clichés."

"You don't believe in it? That organ trafficking?"

"I choose to not entertain the notion."

"What that mean? Not entertain it?"

"I guess you can say I'm in denial."

"Why you take this case if you can't even entertain it? I don't understand that. No disrespect but that's what all this is about so if you don't believe in it we can go ahead and cut this short. I can get back to my chess. I was in the winner seat when you called for me."

"I would like to help. I know this will be a long journey. I am willing to do my best. Whatever it takes. If nothing else I have a daughter so from that aspect I understand at least *why* you did what you did. I understand willing to do anything. For your child."

"Man I ain't denying nothing. Ain't really no need for no lawyer if you wanna know the truth. I'll take whatever time they throw at me. I would do a thousand years for mine. That's just how it is you know?"

"I do."

"So what they want me to say? They think I'm going to lie about it so that's why they sent you? You a public defender right?"

"No."

"No? You ain't no public defender? You a private lawyer? Who sent you? Me and my wife ain't got that type of money for no lawyer. You know I can't pay. I was planning on doing my time since I did the crime. I wasn't asking for no help."

"I was hired to represent you. By that I mean it won't cost you anything. My services have been paid in full. I have been retained to represent you to the best of my ability. That is what I plan to do. So you see it doesn't matter much about what my personal feelings are about this case. I deal strictly on a professional level."

"Wait a minute. Was it Mitch? Did he hire you? You a real professional. You ain't one of them cheap lawyers that take no payments. I bet your retainer real high. Had to be Mitch 'cause he the only one I know can afford services like this."

"No. It wasn't Mitch. And I apologize for this, but I have been asked to keep that generous 'donation' anonymous."

"Is that right?"

"I'm afraid so. If you wouldn't mind I would like to get back to the case. We should go over any evidence acquired during the search of the residence. Anything that will be presented during the trial should be reviewed. It's the history retrieved from your PC."

"What's that?"

"Personal computer. You are entitled to full disclosure of any findings. They have to share any evidence against you when they receive it. There are no secrets between counsel."

"I get it."

"At the time the history was taken of those searches did your family know of Todd's indiscretions? I mean, did you know at that time that he was in another relationship with a man *or* another woman?"

"We didn't have anything concrete. I mean, we knew he wasn't shit, if that's what you really want to know. Same as any other father, we know what some of the cats are up to half the time. Especially if we was into the same thangs. We just older that's all. We didn't know nothing for no fact or nothing. Just that he was making my daughter miserable."

"Take me back. When did you decide that Todd would be a candidate for organ trafficking? Was it before or after your searches?"

"I guess you could say it was at the same time. I ain't never liked the dude. Whole time I was looking that shit up he was on my mind you know what I'm saying? I can't exactly put no finger on it. I guess if you wanna be honest about the shit I always did want him out the picture."

"Can you tell me about Akil Salousamid? What was his role in Todd's disappearance?"

"Who? Who is that? I don't know no Akils man."

"Akil Salousamid was arrested for his involvement in Todd's murder just days after your arrest."

"How is that? Who is that? I don't even know that man Attorney Battle. The man I talked to about all that organ shit was some black dude name David. I don't know nothing about him. Didn't wanna know nothing. He was the only one I talked to and the one who came and gave me that money. Don't even know his last name."

"There were a total of 4 arrests including yours. Of those arrests you were the only African-American. This David was simply a middleman with no clue the seriousness of what he did, meeting with you. Giving you the money."

"I talked to him a few times. Met him at the gym. He seemed cool. 'Bout my age. Said he had daughters and started up this conversation 'bout his problems when we was working out."

"Did you find that odd? That he coincidentally had a similar problem as the one you were having with Cassie?"

"Naw not at the time. Just seemed like he wanted to get some shit off his chest. Wasn't no body else in there lifting weights 'cept me and him so we was lifting weights and talking 'bout shit. I felt what he was saying 'cause I was going through the same type of shit with Cassie."

"And he offered to help with the kidnapping? Did he tell you he knew someone? How did the conversation come about?"

"I told him what I had been thinking about. He told me about his girls, around the same age as Cassandra and I was still tripping about what I seen on YouTube about that shit. All I told him was that it sounded like a good ass plan to get rid of a bad problem I had. I said that would be a good solution if I could find out how to make it happen. Few days later when I seen dude again he told me he could arrange that shit. All he needed to know was where Todd hung at."

"I see now. Did David ever mention Dr. Salous?"

"Dr. Salous? Only Dr. Salous I know of is my wife's doctor. Hell naw we ain't never have no conversations about no doctors. I didn't tell that man none of my business. I met him at the gym. I didn't know him like that man. We just lifted weights together and shit. Spotting each other and shit. I ain't told him shit about my business. 'Specially about my wife. All we talked about was Todd and them niggas his own daughters messed around with. What my wife's doctor got to do with any of this?"

"Akil Salousamid, the man arrested days after you were, practices under the name Dr. Salous. He has been your wife's gynecologist for years."

"Are you kidding me? Dr. Salous? He had something to do with all this? What is you telling me? You telling me that my own wife set me up or something?"

"Please understand. Your wife confided in Dr. Salous during her appointment we can safety presume."

"What? She told him and he did it? He killed Todd or something like that? I ain't the one that killed him so somebody did it. Was it him? She told that I was looking for some cat to kill him? I don't get this shit. Man what is you saying exactly?"

"Needing more information to carry out the plan to sell Todd's organs, Dr. Salous, real name Akil Salousamid, referred her to his colleague. The colleague, also involved in organ trafficking was to act as a therapist to gather more information. Having full access to her demographics from her medical record coupled with his involvement in organ tracking…well it was eventually well known to both men that you would be willing to participate."

"So he sent David to rope me in. I'm black, he black. Same problem with our daughters and no-good ass dudes. Yeah I see how that happened now. Damn, man. Right in front of my face too. That was too much of a coincidence. I didn't even pay the shit no attention neither. Damn, man."

"They followed you. Found out what kind of habits you had, the places you went. After learning you frequented that particular gym, David was hired as the middleman. His job was to join the gym and from that point act as a middleman so you would never know who they were and what they had planned."

"It was a lot of money man."

"Akil Salousamid paid $150,000 for your participation. He paid you for the kidney alone, if you will. In your eyes that was a lot of money and I agree. However, he was compensated way more than that. The transaction was successful. Less the $150,000 you received, he was yet compensated for the liver, heart, brain, and eyes. Imagine what he collected overall."

"A kidney for $150,000? And that man probably killed all kinds of people. Still would be doing it if he didn't get caught. And ain't no telling how long he been doing this shit neither."

"The plan was for you to take the fall for Todd's murder."

"I'm totally shocked right now. I don't know what to say."

"In his line to work, Dr. Salous had access to a lot of potential victims. His patients were women. Women tend to tell stories of abuse a lot of times. When you think more about that woman are willing to tell the entire story regarding what they are going through with their spouses or even sexual harassment at work, happier in their skins if their abuser were taken out of the picture. He would refer the women to what they believed to be therapists. The therapist would get more information for him for monetary gain. I am sure there are more victims at the hands of the good doctor."

"Damn. I'm still tripping on all of this. I can't believe it. Dr. Salous. He was a good doctor. My wife changed a lot after she started seeing him. That miscarriage she had messed her up real bad. He helped her."

"I am sure he was a good doctor. Also a black market affiliated provider. By there being such high demand for healthy organs as you are aware, compensation for a single kidney alone would be enough for an honorable doctor to risk the consequences of being caught."

"May I ask what you did with the money? Cash I am sure."

"Yeah cash money. Crispy bills."

"What did you do with all of the money?"

"I ain't gone say all that Attorney. I will say I needed to get my wife and my daughter – grandbaby - out of Georgia though. Never can be too sure. I was thinking about what if somebody found out about what I did. Come after them? I wasn't gonna have that happen. Same way Todd got taken could happen to them. That shit was real. I found that out when I heard about them finding his body like that, with shit missing. They took that boy's eyes and shit. They had that on the news. Even my wife was a believer after that."

"Did she know you had something to do with the murder at that time?"

"Naw not his murder, nothing like that. She knew about me meeting Dave at the gym and about him telling me he could make it all happen. She told me not to do it. She didn't trust that shit from the word 'Go'."

"She knew it was strange that all of a sudden he had all the players for what you had in mind?"

"You can say that."

"Can I ask why you didn't take heed to how she felt?"

"Yeah you can ask, but I ain't got no good answer. I heard what she said about it being strange. That wasn't nothing new. She was suspicious about a lot of shit. I was focused on my baby. I was thinking about how Cassie would be a lot better when his ass was gone."

"Did she tell you that she had spoken with Dr. Salous at her appointment? She had to have talked to him for you to have even met David in the first place."

"Man she ain't tell me shit about that. That pisses me off she didn't tell me. She didn't tell me 'cause she know I don't like mothafuckas all in my business. Karen know that shit. I don't know why in the world she would've told anybody about that. That was stupid as hell that she did that."

"Do you blame her for all of this?"

"Hell yeah I blame her now that I know all this shit. It all make sense now. Maybe if she told me I could have seen that Dave cat had to be some kinda plant. I would've figured that shit out since somebody else out there knew what I wanted to happen. All of it is some weird shit anyway so as weird as it is, that fit right along with it. Some movie shit. I wish I could talk to her about it. I ain't gone never be able to."

"Why is that?"

"It's over with man. I ain't gone never see them again."

"Whatever time you are sentenced to, Mr. Lancaster, as I stated before, I am willing to do everything as your attorney -"

"Man I took that money and I had them get the fuck away from here. All of 'em. The dog too. I told them I didn't wanna know where they was going. To not even put the house or none of that in their names. I told them don't even contact me in the joint."

"That is a lot to take in. That is a hard pill to swallow."

"It is. They my world. I would love to see how they doing and see the baby grown up. See my beautiful wife and pictures of Cassie graduate from college. Without that mothafucka around I know she would go to college and have a nice career."

"Couldn't they send you pictures? Anonymously?"

"I rather them not do that neither. Don't wanna take no chances at all. Period. I love them just that much, to keep them safe. Even if that means to never see them again, you know what I mean, man. I mean Attorney Battle. A new start somewhere far away where don't no body know them at. In my mind I was laying it down for the rest of my life. They need to live their lives and be safe. That's more important."

"You do understand that you are not being charged with homicide? If anything you may be charged with solicitation. Your arrest is but a small part of a much bigger picture Mr. Lancaster. There are other pieces to this puzzle."

"They trying to find other people that got set up to be murdered? For body parts?"

"Yes they are. At this time there are other residences being searched, evidence has been seized from the offices and residence of Dr. Salous as well as the others involved. There is much more to the story. At the most you could possibly serve time for solicitation, but I believe I can challenge the evidence they will present against you."

"I wish I could let Karen know all this man. She thinkin' I'm going down for murder. Even though I ain't actually kill that cat, man."

"Anything is possible. Perhaps you will be able to see her again one day soon. This case is nationwide Mr. Lancaster. It is unfolding on ABC, CNN, Fox news. You name it. This story is all over the world."

"I am sure it is. Just like the ones I looked up. I seen this story on there, on YouTube, about this boy they found just like that too with his insides totally gone 'cept he was stuffed up with newspaper. Like a dummy or somethin'. Made me look that shit up to read about it. That was too crazy."

"The world news alone could be reason for one's online queries regarding the Black Markets. I mean as opposed to one searching simply for the solicitation of the murder of a bisexual boyfriend I suppose. That could be one reason to search such stories. The mere fact that it is quite unusual could result in such a search."

"Yeah. Sure could."

"You never did tell me. How did you find out Todd was dating both Cassie and your friend Elaine's son Jay?"

"Cassie had a picture. Sent it to my phone. I knew exactly who he was. I didn't tell her that, but I knew who he was soon as I seen it. I called Elaine about it. I knew it. That cat ain't have no business with no picture of a fruitcake in his phone. He had to have been messing with him. I had to call his mama about it soon as I seen it."

"What did you say to her when you called?"

"I started telling her about Cassie. I told her Cassie found that picture of her boy in her baby daddy phone. She was thinking the same thing I was about it. That him and Jay was messing around. Both of 'em was with him. I told her he was my grandbaby's daddy and all that. I said I ain't like the mothafucka and unfortunately that's who he was and all that."

"What was her response to that information?"

"She was in shock. Just like I was. Told me he used to talk to her daughter on the phone when they was younger. She had no idea he had started messing around with her boy. She was 'bout ready to shoot him for that the way she was sounding on the phone. Now that woman don't play no games when it come to her kids. I could just about imagine what was about to happen to the dude after that."

"I know this is a straight-forward question, but did the two of you have a plan to get rid of him? Because of what you had discovered?"

"We didn't discuss nothing like that. I said what I had to say and she said what she had to say. That was it. That was all that was said. She ended up calling me back and told me she went by there to talk to him and some other cats was around there asking about him too. Cassie had put all that shit on the internet before she even sent it to me so I said it was probably somebody trying to put the heat on him 'cause he was gay. You know 'cause it came out that he was messing with another man. Same day he went missing."

"Did she say who they were?"

"Naw. She didn't know who them dudes was. Told me she pointed out who he was when they asked her if she knew him. Guess she saw him over there putting stuff in his car. When that shit came up on the news 'bout him being missing she did say it was on her."

"On her?"

"Yeah. She was thinkin' that she mighta been the one who pointed him out to whoever took him. Same day he went missin'. Wouldn't you think that?"

"Yes I can see her point. Possibly."

"Yeah. Them was probably the cats."

"Is that when you started researching the organs then? After you got the picture from your daughter?"

"Naw, all that was already done. I had already did all that by that time. I found out after the fact that the mothafucka was into all that. That just added to why I didn't like him."

"Elaine does know Cassie, I'm sure, but Cassie and Justin never met? Even though you all had the relationship you did the children never met?"

"Naw the kids didn't know. They hadn't never met each other. Strange thing is we made Elaine and Mitch her godparents. But naw they didn't know. Lemme be honest with you for a minute. Let me share something with you."

"Go ahead. Please."

"Cassandra didn't live with us."

"What do you mean? Where did she live?"

"She stayed with Karen's mama."

"You speaking about – what time period did she reside with her grandmother? She had an apartment with Todd am I correct?"

"Yeah they stayed together. I'm talking about coming up. She ain't live with us coming up. She lived at Karen mama house. She lived with her. It's like this, Attorney. I ain't her real daddy. Cassandra ain't biologically my daughter."

"You adopted her? She did reside with you and your wife as an infant correct?"

"Found out before she was a year old she wasn't even mine. It hurt man. All that beggin' I did, asking Karen to have that baby for me when I found out she was pregnant. I just knew she was pregnant by me man. You know I never got a chance to raise my son all the way up. I found out when we met she was still involved with that man but the way it all went down I wasn't thinking no shit like that happened."

"What did happen? Did you know what their situation was at that time?"

"Yeah I knew she was in a bad situation. They was still under the same roof and all that, but they was in the process of breaking up.

We moved kinda quick man that's all that was. I was with her 'bout a week after I met her."

"Did they continue having a relationship after you two were together?"

"Not long after that the cat moved on out of they apartment they had. Obviously they did a little something around that time. Me and her thought the baby was mine though. We was getting down on a regular basis so I guess we assumed it was me when she took the test. When he left I moved on in."

"Ok I understand now."

"I was hurt. Karen was hurt. Seemed like the best thing to do was to let her mama raise her when we found out."

"How did you find out exactly?"

"Cassie always did look mixed to me. I'm black as hell. Her mama damn sure black as hell. Cass ain't all black. Man I knew she couldn't have been all black the way her hair was and how light she was. No features of mine's or Karen's. She ain't never get no color like Karen said would happen. She kept saying Cassie was going to get darker. Guess not if she wasn't mine. That other cat wasn't all black. He had some type of Mexican in him. I was in denial about it at first. Then I had to accept it and get the test done."

"DNA proved that Cassie was biracial?"

"Yep that's exactly what it said. That wasn't nothing you couldn't tell by looking. Unless you trying not to see that shit."

"That is – some news. Cassandra is still Cassandra Lancaster correct?"

"Yeah man. She STILL my daughter. I don't care about no test. I was there when she was born. I was up in the middle of the night giving her that bottle. Karen over there knocked out and I'm up with the baby damn near all night."

"You both decided it would be best if Karen's mother raise her? When did you decide that would be better. How old was she?"

"She was about – probably 2-years-old by then. Naw it was before that. Before her birthday came around again. We didn't have no lot of money back then and both of us wanted the best for her. We didn't have no real nice spot to stay at. Her mama got a real nice house and that cat lived there so yeah. She took her."

"The cat lived there? Which cat are you referring to? Are you speaking of Cassandra's father?"

"Yeah. He lived there. You ok man? Attorney Battle? You cool man?"

"Wait a second. I am ok. That information was – alarming. Cassandra's biological father lives with Karen's *mother*?"

"Yeah he do. That's where he moved out to when they broke up. He her stepson."

Chapter 7: Miss Busy Body

I was glad her daddy got involved and went and got her. I don't know who called him up but I sure am glad somebody did. Didn't none of us know where she disappeared off to chile! Just up and left one day. That house she had over there had gotten sold off so where was she laying her head at? She wasn't in no jailhouse 'cause she didn't get in no trouble behind that Charles dying the way he did. That was all settled. And we settled it. She ran as fast as she could to get away from all that 'ole mess she had going on over there. She was able to hide them hands about that Charles chile and that secret was one that wouldn't never be told. I can't say I blame her for it, but we was worried about that girl. At least she could've talked some to her daddy, let him know where she was living at least.

Even he knew she wasn't well no more. That weak soul needed God's hands on her to nurse her back to health. What if that po' chile decided she needed to hurt somebody else? Well I don't think she would need to do that, but what if she did? No body had no answers for that. If anybody could help her it was her daddy. Wasn't no way in the world he would have let that girl run around here suffering the way she was, chile, no way in the world!

All that time she was gone we all was sitting around worried to death about her! It had been a long time since she had been 'round any of us. The way she felt about Kennedy I couldn't believe the last time she played with her was during the holiday. We was all together under the same roof on that Christmas Eve. We spent the holidays out at Mick's house. All of us was celebrating there together as a matter of fact. Tawana had stopped coming around as much as she used to when her mama was livin', but we did get to lay eyes on her some of the time. I didn't know if she was planning on joining us or not 'cause she never did answer her phone. She came on out there.

From what I found out she had taken up with some fella. We hadn't never heard who he was or what his job was nothing like that. Not even what color he was either. All we knew was that she was always shacked up with him whoever he was, and he lived right here in Georgia. Figured he must've been the fella she was dating 'round with when she walked in that front door. Chile that man was so close to her he might as well been the scarf hanging from her neck. He was obviously taken with that big 'ole butt on the back of her because all he did was brush up against her as she was introducing him to all of us. When he wasn't touching on her back and rubbing up against her there she was perched up on his lap and carrying on. It wasn't no secret she was probably high on something or 'nother 'cause that Tawana wasn't one to be kissing all on no body. "Specially in front of her daddy. She might as well been still a little girl when Mitch was around. That didn't bother her none, kissing on that man in the mouth for all of us to take in. And the way she was with germs just like her mama was, that surprised me some that she was doing that in the first place. Umph, chile, believe me, I was shocked!

That was a good thing for her besides all of that. I was happy for her. That baby found her somebody to put that smile back on her face where it needed to be. Going through hell like she was. I sure was happy for her.

I called him Dr. Victor. Didn't catch what his last name was. Too hard for me to say one of them Jewish names so I settled with that. Him and Jason spent a great deal talking back and forth 'bout stuff I don't know about. Doctor talk I called it. Most of all he was a big improvement as far as the eye could see and mighty fascinated with her and watching her every move. Enjoyed all the food too. Looked like it was something he could get used to. It was his first time eating collard greens. All he was used to was salads and the only ham he had ever tasted was named Honeybaked. Looked a ways younger than she was but that was ok nowadays. These women loved to date a younger man. Them younger men put that spark back in them I heard. He was a white man too. Tawana had landed herself a doctor.

That part of it didn't surprise me none. She was working at that hospital! That's where all the doctors are chile honey, in that hospital. All them hours she was working and how she was always made up so pretty and looking so neat in them scrubs she wore I expected that eventually. He looked pretty friendly and she was just as friendly. I could tell he wasn't no type that would place his hands on a woman the wrong way. That is the change she needed. Them black men like to use intimidation. Some of 'em wanna beat they woman half to death 'cause they either jealous you doing something or just plain 'ole insecure of they own self. That's how my ex was. Chile that man was hitting me upside my head like he was crazy and just out the blue. After I took that skillet and knocked him upside his head to see how he liked it I made sure I put his ass on the other side of my door. Didn't look back. When that oldest boy made up in his mind that he was going to be just like him at only 11 years old, didn't matter none to me to send him right out the door behind him. No Lord I was not putting up with that nonsense.

Tawana looked mighty good that last time. Better than she had been looking so I didn't suspect a thing. Her hair was slicked back in a bun at least and not all over her head. Her face looked different to me but that was just a small wonder. She was just so giggly tending to that man I fell in love with how she was so happy in that moment. Lord I wish I had've known Dr. Victor was busy introducing her to a new habit. No wonder she was so giggly when not a thing was funny. It was him. He was writing all them prescriptions and giving them to her like it wasn't never gone be found out. It's consequences to anything you do in the dark or light.

I thought them doctors made a lot of money. Why would he need to have her helping him sell them pills like that? It was obvious that they was going right into Tawana's mouth and his mouth too. They was both hooked on them pills, making all that money down there selling them prescriptions and carrying on. They lived like that for a good while behind the scenes. He the one she had been seeing when her and Charles was on the rocks, getting prescriptions to help her through it. She had them Vicodin pills and the rest of 'em too I'm sure. Had a good feelin' that's what was a help to her to ease some of that pain she had going on with that cheating man of hers she was married to. She was able to get her some diff'rent type of love going on. I didn't know the deal behind all that smilin' so I was busy smilin' wit her. Umh. Po Tawana.

Bank account had to be spent all up. Tawana was the last one had to live the way she was, in that downtown area down there. It wasn't the east side of town with all them criminals, but it wasn't safe to be walking the street if you ask me about it. You can still drive past that part of town and see the homeless laying out in the open. Time to time you may see a hooker or two standing there. I wouldn't be able to call it a home that's for sure.

Shock to me to know that's where she had been hiding herself for all that time. Guess we wouldn't have known where she was. Ain't never no reason to go on down there. They ain't finished trying to fix it up yet. They planning on making it better down there in the future. The apartments she was staying in was called condominiums. Wasn't like no condos the white folk with a little money buy up. These places was fancy enough, but they wasn't no real condominiums. Them was apartments. Prolly most they had in them was fireplaces or something like that. Charging all that rent 'cause they called them condominiums.

When I heard that she was down there living like that, looking unkept with her hair all cut off, it was a shame! Here it was her very own siblings were living like a king and queen in they own rites with the richest beauty shop in all Georgia and she running around like that, like a vagrant. It was unbelievable. Ump! A shame! Didn't wanna do nothin' no more after her mama died. Even Cobi tried to reach out to her and let her live there with her and that baby and she didn't even wanna do that. That chile cut her phone completely off after that. Then she was gone. Disappeared.

Them kids had it in they mind that maybe she could work up in that shop with them, help her get out that funk she fell off into. Figured all of 'em could be 'round each other if she did that, 'cause all of 'em was sad not just her. Justin is so smart! He was all ready to pay that money to that school so she could learn how to do hair with them. It was set up already chile. The application was done and he was 'bout ready to get her a place right there near that shop. She wouldn't hear of it. Told Cobi on that phone to tell him 'No!' Said it wasn't no way she was doing no hair. She wasn't doing no hair after she was a nurse all that time. That was something that was belittling to her somehow or another which didn't make not a lick of sense. She was on drugs and was a nurse. That should have been way more of an embarrassment if you ask for my opinion. Oh well. They went on and left it alone. Wasn't no more nurse money coming in the door no more so that was totally on her if she didn't want to take it as a way to pull herself up by the boot straps. Of course that probably wasn't the only thing about it. She may have felt some type of ways that it was her baby brother's idea to rescue her as old as she was and should have known better than to be down like she was.

She didn't want to stay in the house with me. When she called me up to ask about coming to get some of Elaine's things I told her on the phone 'Come on, come stay here with Cat, I help you much as I can baby, Cat got 'cha.' That's what I always tole the kids. After I said that it felt just like I had cursed her in some way when I said it. I guess it was a bad idea that Mick pick her up and bring her straight to me. She didn't wanna get out of the truck at all. Wasn't thinking too much when I came up with the idea. Her mama had died in the house so I understood that. Prolly was exactly the root of why all this had gone on in the first beginning. Lord! I had to tell the Lord I was sorry 'bout bringing all them memories back to her mind, whatever she had left after them drugs. I just waved at 'em both as they pulled on away from the curb. Was snowing so bad I couldn't see if they had even waved back or not.

Yeah we all knew 'bout the hard stuff she was into by that time. It started off being pills and all that drinking that old hard liquor. I can tell ya exactly how I found out she was hooked on that heroin. Emily told me all about it. I useta play bingo every week. That's all I had going on was the church house and my bingo for seven years straight. The last few years I was at that bingo parlor near the house. In fact I made a few big bucks playing bingo at that one. Was hooked after that. Winning that game one Friday evening was enough to buy me that big TV I kept dreaming about. I wanted all the hookups on it. I needed to get that, what you call it? Hulu, Netflix, a fire stick…you know that thing that's out now, where you can watch all the movies. I love me some movies! I ain't know how to do all that though so I had to call Curtis to help me hook it all up. Lord knows he be so busy all the time I gotta make an appointment to get some help from my own son.

Anyway I made fast friends with this dear heart called Effie. Now Effie wasn't that old. She was round in her late forties, maybe 50 I would guess. She never did win too much but somethin' is always way better than nothin'.

Chile, Miss Effie's baby girl was called Emily. Emily was a real name but Miss Effie said that was her play name. A play name at 32? Yes ma'am, the real name was almost from her mama Effie. Effimalaye Ladonna. What in the world? You could tell in that way she WAS off a bit. Was that some sorta African name? I asked her. What does it stand for? The story she told was that she was sick when she had her early. Had some blood pressure issues and it caused Emily to be born early. By her being in housekeeping wasn't no way she could work and no way she could take off all that time and get some money for it neither. It was what was called a double edge sword I suppose.

The doctor had told her that if she got some paperwork he could sign 'em and she would be alright for that time off. You know, that she could still have her job when she got back and if there was money in her sick time bank she could most prob'ly take all of it and still have a job to go back to.

"He told me to go to my job and get some FMLA papers. At first I couldn't make out what he was talking about so he explained it some more. Some law was in place that helped you out when you had to work but was too sick to go. The Family and Medical Leave law." She told me.

She was chewing like some slow cow, smacking on something that must've been made straight in Heaven. Lord knows I was trying to be patient, listening for the part that would explain what all that had to do with Emily.

"Well I wasn't gone be able to pay no rent with no check coming. I didn't know what I was gonna do. I had a new little baby, weighing only 3 pounds at that time and we was barely making it as it was. How was I gonna take off from my job and take care of my baby? Doctor Johnson said that paper was my answer for it. That's what her name was gone be. That was my saving grace! I didn't never like the name Grace so I picked the otha one."

We was both quiet for a while. Lord knows I didn't want to ask her. I didn't understand one bit of it at all. All I could do was nod my head. Must've read that right off my face that I wasn't takin' none of it in.

"F-M-L-A. *Effimalaye*. We all just call her Emily 'cause it is way easier."

That was the end of that. Never did ask her no more questions. I just plain didn't wanna know nothing else 'bout her logic. I didn't need to know no more 'bout how she was thinking.

Bingo was Emily's game like it was mine. She was there with her mama every Friday evening. Prolly to make sure wasn't no body getting over on poor Effie. She needed that extra help. I sure declare. Lord knows that girl reminded me so much of Tawana. She was the kinda girl Tawana needed as a friend 'stead of that mousy girl. Didn't seem to me like she was for no mess, always hanging close near her mama and didn't have no chil'ren neither just like Tawana. They was close in age. Honestly it was my plan to make them friends. I called Miss Effie for her and Emily to come on by and watch some movies and had cooked somethin' up to snack on. I was plannin' on Tawana coming by to get her a break from sitting with Kennedy for a spell. When they got there we was sitting there waitin' on her and talking 'bout this and a little of that, me and Emily, and she started telling me about her daddy. He had a strange name too she shared with me. Wasn't just her with the weird name, she wanted me to know. Stanford was at least a *regular* name even if was kinda nerdy. They just called him 'Stan' so that wasn't too nerdy I laughed with her. Too bad she ain't get no regular name like him.

Tawana ain't never show up so we went on and watched the movie without her. Still turned out to be a nice time. I had been wanting to see that Black Panther movie since I seen the previews last year so when I seen it was out I was all ready for it. Too bad she missed it 'cause that one man was one of her favorite actors, that Michael B. Jordan. She didn't have no phone to get in touch with her so I called up Cobi to see if she was at the house. She hadn't heard from her since the night before she said. Last she seen her she was laying in the bed and said she was having some kinda pains. She assumed like I did that it was withdrawal from all them drugs she was missin'. I know her daddy went and picked her up from her cousin's house where she had been hidin for a few years.

Wasn't no way she had did no drugs when she was around Mick so she was at least dry for some time. Maybe it was when she got the chance to be alone she felt the need to go scare up some type of high. Course she wouldn't have done that around her daddy. I wish he made the decision to keep her on with him 'steada givin' her a voice in it. Mick had some type of way with keeping that respect he was due. Either that or they just didn't want they daddy mad at 'em for nothing in the world. All of 'em had a special place in his heart. Specially her. She needed it the most. Anyway if we was dead on she had been clean for a little while at least. I still hadn't layed one eye on her yet.

"I wasn't gone leave Kennedy with her since she sick. I got her with me. Did you call the house phone?" She asked me.

"Naw I didn't. I shoulda did that first. I'm so used to calling your cell phone girl."

She ain't never been the type to answer no ringing phones. That girl gets on my nerves not answering the phone. Oh well. Guess she just gone miss the movie. I bet she wasn't never even planning on showing up anyway.

"Maybe on the next go round you can meet her Emily. She must got a lot going on today. Least she coulda did was call." I explained to her.

I never did do no redecorating since Elaine passed on to glory. Emily couldn't help it none but see the kids' pictures hangin' up on the walls. She saw her face sure enough. A lot of us can't help but know some of the same people rather you kin to 'em or just run in the same circles as people do. Recognized her face on the picture on the way to the kitchen. Good thing it happened like that, that she asked for another slice of my sweet potato pie. Just as sure as I'm a black woman Emily already did know who Tawana was. She lived right in the same place as her daddy lived at. She told me a whole lot more than I bargained for, Lord have mercy. She sure did! Not only did she know her she knew all about the man she been carrying on with for that time she been missing. When we ain't know what she had been up to she was livin' down there and was no wheres near the Tawana we was used to. Chile honey I called everybody I could think of as soon as they left that house.

It was some type of intervention they did over at that church with her, trying to get her to get on the right pathway. That wasn't workin' not a bit. Them mothers of the church got a hold of her and whilst one was designated to feed her 3 square meals every day the others were showing up with all types of pies and homemade candies. When they weren't praying over her she was stuck in church surrounded by all of them trying to keep her mind off all that devilish behavior. Lord knows that chile was losing her mind.

Good thing she ain't bring no chil'ren in the world, her and Charles before he left here. That woulda been a shame. For both of 'em. He had a problem with that drinkin' and she was suffering from these here drugs. Wasn't just her. It was some epidemic, that all these young folk can't help but be taken over by all the pills and shooting up and carrying on. I know it's always been a thing going on even back in my days but lately folks dropping like flies! Never did think in my wildest dreams it would be one of them kids. No Lord I sure didn't.

I had figured on the church women to have a good hold on her. It was a lot of 'em. You know they was dedicated to they church. Ain't none of 'em have no full time commitment to work. A few of 'em worked at Walmart and at the grocery for a few hours but the full time job was owed to they God. Would do whatever it took to take care of one of God's shepherds. Mick was God's shepherd, with him pitching the Lord's word ev'ry Sunday and sometimes even on Wednesday nights. I went to all of the services, you know. Anyhow doing God's work meant helping with his daughter too. That was helping with Tawana and all her issues so Mick could carry on with his Word he had to deliver to folks. All us felt like that was a great idea so many eyes could be focused on her at one time. Sometimes they was even able to keep an eye or two on her.

She still did manage to get away. When she came back she was always quiet and to herself. Mother Johnnie Mae said she was up to somethin' just like her grandbaby used to be so she knowed it wasn't right whatever it was. I can't exactly put a finger on it, but if you was to ask me she got back out there and had some drugs to make her feel better.

Chapter 8: Calvin

I gots to find me a new spot to get my hair cut and shit. Been at that job for a little while now. Ain't no other brothas in there. Only me. I can't be up in there lookin' crazy. I gots to represent all the otha brothas they won't ever know. They need to see all of us ain't all bad. Last time I went up in The Sharp Edge and all my boys – all them niggas who use to be my boys - was in there lookin' at me like I did something to them and shit. That was the first time I been in there that late. I ain't have no choice that day. I had to go after work because I promised my moms I could help her out with the yard. That was gone be an all day thang so shit. I figured I might as well go 'head and go get my hair cut up after work. That's when all my boys be in there. E*specially* on Fridays getting ready for that weekend.

All I did was move outta that part of town and it was almost like we wasn't boys no more, like I had robbed one of them how they kept sizing me up. That's how it is in the hood. You can't act like you want to improve on how you livin'. That's what they call a sin. Almost like being in the other gang fa real.

I ain't on all that shit no more. Straight as an arrow now. I'm too damn old for that gang shit. I don't need no problems. Sittin' here lookin' at my phone, puttin' in dif'rent zip codes seeing what shops around where I'm at now. I'm from the Points so I ain't familiar with over here yet. Everything I had to do was always in the Points, you know? I found a slick spot up on Grandolph alright. That spot is right by that mall where I be seeing shorty at. I done seen her once or twice passing through there so yeah. I need to slide through there and check it out one day sooner than later and then I can hit up that mall. Might as well. Wasn't nothing going on lately.

Job is real cool but I ain't got no more social life. Social life been gone down the tubes since my girl left me. I had so much money left after my bills 'cause she gone. I ain't have no girl to spend it on no more. I miss her though. A lot. I admit it. If she wasn't on that shit, we coulda worked out. I wanted to marry that fox. She was the one for me I was thinking. I was thinking wrong then. We was on the outs when she up and left so deep down its cool. I think it is man, I guess it woulda been a bad choice to stay with her because she was too gone. I thought about all of it. I was in process of trying to figure out if I wanted to let her go when she came to me and said she was out. Said it wasn't working out and she had to move on. I done heard that shit before, 'bout moving on. That mean she got another nigga somewhere that she been creeping around with, that's what that shit mean. Wasn't nothing 'bout no not getting along. Who do really get along shit? I don't know no couple that's perfect.

She got all her shit and she left. Tomorrow makes 2 damn years since she left on January 25th. Waited good until I pulled out for work my neighbor told me. This nosey cat name Stan watch over thangs while people at work. He retired and shit so he ain't got nothing else to do but sit around watchin' people's shit for them. Dude told me that she left out in some green truck. Said some man helped her put her shit in the back of it and took off all in under 5 minutes. Couldn't tell me what the cat looked like. It was snowing and shit so he had on a hat and a big ass coat. The truck was one of them new ones so he had some big money. She was on drugs real bad so I had it in my mind that it wasn't no good thang she was up to.

I ain't even seen her since that morning she took off. No kiss bye or nothing. I came home and the only shit there was my shit. Some of it. It wouldn't be her if she didn't take something, I know man. Some of my sneakers were gone. The boxes too. Never could have no change jar sitting out in the open. I had to hide my shit in a Quaker oats container on the kitchen shelf. *That* container was gone. She found my shit.

I think it was about a month…probably around that, before old girl left she told me some stuff 'bout herself. I don't know why she waited til we had been kickin' it for all that time knowing she was leaving the whole time to tell me shit. Whole time I didn't know too much about her. Just a little bit about her folks. She mentioned her sister and her brothers but that's it though. Never about where they lived at or what they did for a living and all that. She was a nurse so pretty sure they had good jobs and shit too. I didn't know nothing about her other than that. That's how she was though. She was a quiet girl, man, never said too much. Then on top of it she was on them drugs so her moods was all up and down. One minute she all sleepy and nodding off, then she wake up and start cleaning up all of a sudden or put YouTube on like she was always doing and watch videos, dancing around. I never could get used to it, them personalities she keep changing back and forth.

She never did look me in my eyes no more but she was looking right at me and acting real strange telling me all about her family. Guess she was too damn high to keep her mouth shut and needed to get it out. Man she told me some real deep shit. Shit that I would never repeat you understand what I'm telling you? Ain't never heard nothing about none of it and when she finally do let it out it seem like it's out of some movie. The way she was talking her family just like the mafia. Seem like no matter what happen they help you fix that shit. We was sitting in the bed after we had did our thing and she was just flowing.

My lady told me 3 dif'rent stories about people that done came up missing and ain't no body do a day in prison. Shit would happen and they would keep they mouths shut and that was it. That was they rule. If that had've been me back in the day I woulda been up under some prison. All I had my whole life was my mama and we didn't have no money. We was average people. Blue collar family you could call us. Wasn't nothing special about me and my mama. We didn't have it like her daddy did and her mama. She let me know that they had it going on and family meant everything at whatever cost. They took care of they own. And they had money to make problems go away was what she was telling me.

I didn't have no body to help me get out of the sticky situations I ever had going on. It ain't never been no rapes or no homosexual instances like she was telling me about had happened in her family. It wasn't no abuse or nothing so that was the difference. All I ever got myself in was sellin some blow or some herb in the street. Didn't nothing compare to what she been through man. I know I was all in her mouth I was so interested in what she was talking about. I felt like I was sitting in the front row at the theater. She was fine as hell with no makeup on her face so I couldn't help staring right at her. She was naked from me and her getting down so that made it more interesting to me. She had her little cigarette and puffing her ass off just talking. Baby was on a roll!

Some parts of what she was telling me I can't even say I believed all of it, like her telling me about her little sister getting raped and how she ended up killing the dude. That was prolly her imagination from all them drugs messing her brain up. I knew that shit couldn't be true 'cause there was no way she could get away with something like that. She started talking like she was some assassin. I ain't believe none of that part of it, but it sounded kind've true about them paying people for beat downs. I could see that fa real.

 I had a dif'rent type feeling about how I needed to deal with her after she told me all that. I ain't gone say I was scared…let's just say I was glad she liked me, let's just say that. That had to be the reason them drugs got her after I found out about all that crazy shit. That lady had been through a LOT. A lot of it *she* did *herself.*

She got fired for stealing pills out of the nurses' station 'round when we moved in together. All those years of school down the goddamn drain. Her mama was proud of her becoming a nurse like she was and getting a good job after she graduated. Her Daddy was too. I heard he was some big preacher in Chicago bragging on his daughter from the pulpit a lot of Sundays. Bet he would've had a fucking heart attack and turned in his robe if he knew that perfect Tawana of his went from being a nurse to a pill-popping nurse to using fentanyl. After using it for so long I guess that wasn't even doing it for her. She started mixing that shit with that heroin. I didn't know where she was getting the money to buy that shit after she lost her job until my shit started coming up missing. I would take my shower and be in my closet trying to find my Jordans and they gone. $250 Jordans I ain't never took out the shoebox…GONE. I still never found my daddy's class ring, my Levi's or my gold chain. The shit got ridiculous man.

I asked her one time, "Tee, why you always wanna get *high*?"

I thought she was running away from something. Trying to drown out something in her life that was bothering her.

"'Cause I can't stop. It feels so *good*." She sang.

Her eyes rolled back in her head and shit. I thought that's how she felt when I was banging her, but she was sitting her skinny ass up there talking about getting blowed, getting high.

"You just don't know what you missin', to feel like you're up in the clouds for a little while before you have to come back down here again. To real life. It feels so peaceful. Your body is so *calm. Relaxed*."

That bitch was CRAZY dog. She was some type of lunatic. This chick was moving her arms in the air like she was a damn bird, swinging her head and shit. I didn't know what the fuck she *meant* by all of that. What the hell was she talking about? Is that what it was for *her*? Because that ain't how the fuck it was for *me*. Coming in from work every day, which somebody had to do 'cause her ass didn't work no where, and have to check your woman out to see if she was still breathing or not. That ain't no feeling of peace to *me*. Yeah she was right, the body IS calm. Real calm. That was what in the fuck made me think she was laying there dead from an overdose, all them pills she was taking. Or that shit she was putting in her veins. I come in from work and she drooling at the mouth, barely able to keep her eyes open. Every time I would see her like that, my next move after making sure she was alive was to see how she managed to get that way. Find out what was missing out the house, see what ring she pawned that I gotta get out. I wasn't just gone watch her lose her mama's rings. Her mama dead. That ain't cool.

She was my dream come true first few months. When I got hired over at Richmond and Associates, I had to make a change in my environment too not just my job, where I worked. I found out real quick I didn't belong over there in the Points. It was time for me to leave that thug life alone altogether. Them niggas was up all night drinking and throwing dice. Outside at 2, 3 in the morning cussing and smoking weed. I never could get a good night's sleep. I had to move. I had to.

It was nice over there. Wasn't that far from work and it was by the water and shit. Had 2 bedrooms and a fireplace. I ain't never had no crib like that. First few days I had to stare out the window every time I walked by it, 'cause it hadn't sunk in yet how easy it was to be legit. My car was parked in a *carport*. I had all the loot they asked for to rent it out and my credit wasn't as bad as I thought it would've been. Hadn't never used it for nothing. I always paid cash. I didn't have nothing that I needed to have a credit score to get. I was excited as hell when they called and said I could move in. Right on time. I had a good week before the job even started. Things was going my way. I had a new gig sorting mail and delivering it around the office and all I needed was some special lady to share all that with.

I kept seeing her. She came home in nurse clothes and after that I'm looking at her laying out next to the pool. She was a foxy ass lady. I wanted to get to know her after I seen her two or three times. I ain't have no woman no more so I was down with it. Last time I was even with a woman was my baby mama and she had a new dude in the picture. It was time for me to move on myself. I didn't just want no booty calls. I wanted a relationship with a new lady. With her. She could nurse me back to health any time I made sure I let her know. It worked. For a minute we couldn't get enough of each other. I was happy and she looked like she was happy. Until it was obvious I couldn't have been making her too happy for her to want some other kind of high than the one I was giving her.

Later on I found out that the same night we slept together for the first time, she stole some pills before she got off work. She tried to say she was nervous about being with me for the first time, but she wasn't no fucking virgin. She used to fuck the doctor she was working for, she told me. And it didn't matter whether they had patients or not. If he wanted it, they would go right in that office and then she would take a shower in his bathroom and put her scrubs back on. She wasn't no saint. That nervous shit she told me was a lie. She was taking pills because that's what the hell she wanted to do. Ain't have shit to do with me. I was in love with her by the time I found out she was hooked, gone off it. We was supposed to been moving towards marriage. Until her addiction, they call it, got fuckin' worse.

I hadn't met none of her family. They needed to come help her wherever they was hiding or she needed to quit hiding from them. She didn't want to listen to me. Said she could stop when she was ready to stop and she wasn't ready. What addicts you know admit they can't stop using? We was having a baby a few months back and she had a miscarriage at 3 months pregnant. Hurt me to the core. Always getting high and killed my baby. Her being pregnant didn't mean nothing to her but it meant everything to me. I wasn't allowed to see my daughter since her moms was done with me so when that test turned out positive that was another chance for me to get to be a dad. A good dad this time. Then she killed my baby.

I wasn't gonna say shit you feel me? The shit she was doing and how her family was, all prestigious and shit maybe they didn't need to know. I was positive I was keeping that shit under wraps. Especially if she could change. I couldn't bring myself to tell Foxy to leave. Days kept going on and on and I couldn't let her go. I was indecisive all the way 'til she let me know it was a done deal. That's crazy ain't it? Almost brought a brotha to tears to walk in like they do on the movies and the drawers she used was all empty with hangers on the floor in the closet like somebody done robbed my crib. Standing there man looking at that shit when Stan knock on my door with the news. Told me what he seen. That fucked me up something awful. I mean that messed me up bad.

On what woulda been our 2nd anniversary - coincidentally the day
she left - I owed it to myself to check out that new spot. It was
Saturday morning and I was laying there thinking 'bout her. Today
was the day we was supposed to kick it. Celebrate knowing each
other. She was supposed to have on my ring that day, getting ready
to be my wife, my queen. I got on up and got me some breakfast.
Fixed me some pancakes and eggs. A little bacon and shit. I get
there, to the new spot. You know for my haircut. I was still feeling
down, man. I hadn't even seen my ex fox in a long while. I walk in
there man, and I'll be Goddamn man. You will never believe it. My
girl's picture was hanging up in the fucking lobby.

Chapter 9: Justin the Great

Didn't not none of us know who he was honey. The whole second floor was looking at that tall sexy ass in the dead center of my lobby. Sad desperate people too, honey, because it was a good 10 other customers waiting in line and not one of us gave a damn about any of them paying customers. No, child, we had our eyeballs set and focused on the likes of him! All of us had our eyes glued on that security camera. As a matter of fact it was a damn good thing we had the camera in the first place thanks to Miss Cobi's scary ass. Little thing wanted it so we could see what was going on honey even though all the doors to each floor stayed locked up. Here we all was using it to be nosy! Shame on all of us.

He said his name was Calvin or somebody. Honey he was fine. Came in here to get a cut. Clean face and tall. Real tall just like I like my mens. I had never laid eyes on him before. Linnie said he was down in the lobby staring at my sister's picture. Child she said he looked so confused! Yeah I sure did have her picture up there on my memorial wall but honey that's because we buried that old Tawana. Honey we put that drugged up Tawana to rest and buried her way down under never to return again. She was *almost* dead honey. *Almost.* But we wasn't about to go there any longer. All that is done and long over with. I wanted my big sister's picture down there front and center honey! Dead. Child *please.* Tawana ain't no dead!

That is exactly why I sent Jacobi right up to that third floor to find out about him. Child I ain't about to take no chances. I refuse to take not one chance with anything honey. It be a lot going on these days. I wish I might let some thug walk up into my place of business and start a bunch of trash. Well I don't know if 'thug' is the correct adjective or if it's not a good description, but that is neither here *nor* is it there. Bottom line is that I don't know if it is the case or not a case at all. That is what I need to get to honey. We real protective around here. Everyone is friendly and all but - and every one of us got one of those - it seem a lot to me like he waltzed in here off the street looking for that child.

Ain't no telling what Tawana was into all them years she was hiding out. He could've been somebody looking for her for some old drug debt, we didn't have no way of knowing all that honey and that was something we needed to know! Who in all of Georgia didn't know me and Miss Cobi was siblings to her? Google honey, Google. You can look anything up nowadays. You can type in any address right on the laptop and look dead at the house they livin' in!

All we wanted to know was what his story was. Was he some old boyfriend she had? Last man we knew of was that white doctor fella she was always with after Charles died. That was around the time she fell on off. After that man got arrested and sent up the river her mentality went afloat right after him. That doctor was her clutch honey! She lost everything she had trying to keep up with that lifestyle he led her into. This one had to have come after all that. He fit in there somewhere.

Linnie told us he was asking what happened to the girl on the picture and if she had something to do with the shop. That question could have been wondering if she owned it. Read between those lines. You can't put nothing past no body. If she did own it that could be a pretty payment for some old debt. I thinks about all that stuff like that. Some family gets killed because of some weak link in the family being too messy to keep themselves straight. Done seen a movie or two where that has been the case. I can't think of the names of none of them movies, honey, but you know what I'm talking about. You seen some of 'em too at some point or another.

I wasn't planning on being brash. That was the whole reason for sending Miss Cobi up there to get something out of him. She knew how to get it done honey. I just ain't got no more patience at this age to be playing with folk. She get in that different role than the one I step into honey, especially when it come to my family and my money.

Child she felt all she needed was that little 22. I guess it wasn't as big a threat in her mind like I was thinking about it. She put that thing in the back of her pants and put that headset in her pocket. Ain't nan one of us been packing with that little thing in years and that's what she felt comfortable taking up there to talk to that strange man. She crazy as hell. What if he had a piece on *him*? Never can tell nowadays is all I'm saying. I guess if it all did go down it wasn't no way he was getting out of here in one piece no way. I guess I was greatly over exaggerating honey. I needed to calm down 'cause she didn't waste not one minute going to see him face-to-face. She was up on that 3rd floor already talking to him while I was still trying to figure out how to approach him with all the questions. Ain't that something? She good ain't she honey?

"Hey, how are you today? Welcome to The Wild Hair. How you like it so far?"

"It's nice. *Real* nice. You the official greeter?"

"Naw I'm no greeter. How did you hear about us… umm, I'm sorry. I didn't catch your name -"

"It's fine little mama, I didn't throw it. My name Calvin. I'm just checking out new places in the area since I moved out this way. Hope that's ok with you Miss Lady. And who might you be? You the one cutting my hair today?"

"Not today Calvin. Maybe next time. Actually you in line for Chad. Chad is one of the best. You in good hands."

"How is that determined, ah, what is your name now?"

"My name Jacobi. I'm one of the owners here. And how we set up here is we have our barbers on this floor - the third floor - and down on the second is where the ladies – and some *men* – get their hair done. Weaves, braids, natural hairstyles, you know. First floor is shampoos and relaxers. Dyes. By the way, if you get hungry you can stop down in the cafeteria. Good food down there. You should check it out!"

"Yeah, I think I may become one of your regulars if you'll have me. I like this setup. It's nice. Feels like home. I see y'all got pictures all throughout the shop. I seen one of you hanging up as a matter of fact. Family pictures?"

"Yes they *are.* Those are all pictures of me and my family. Family is everything you know. Do you have any questions Calvin?"

"As a matter of fact I'm glad you asked. I do have a question. I happen to know someone in one of the pictures – in the lobby. The big picture. I know that young lady. The fox…uhh she used to be a dear *dear* friend of mine. We lost touch. I happen to come in on a whim and see that she…I didn't know she had passed. Man, damn. When did she uhh…damn. I didn't even know she had -"

"Don't trip! Tawana fine. It's ok. You ain't the first one who thought she was dead. She fine. Thas my big sister. My brother started this shop. He had his reasons for wanting her picture up there like that. We gone just blame Justin for that."

"Man, that got me trippin, I ain't gonna lie. I might have to go have me a drink after that one. You got me Shorty. My mind went somewhere else when I heard that. Wasn't expecting that shit. My bad. Excuse my language Shorty."

"Imma make sure you meet him so you can yell at him for that. Looks like that upset you a little bit. Y'all musta been real dear friends, hunh? She ok. Her and the baby don't live in Georgia no more 'cause she wanted a fresh start. That's probably why y'all lost touch. They live in Ohio now though. That's why ain't no body seen her in a while. You ok?"

"Her *baby*??? She had a baby? Man. I didn't know that. What she have? Girl? Boy? That's amazing. A *baby*? When that happen?"

"What you mean, 'when that happen'? Well if I had to guess, she was pregnant for 9 months and little John John just turned 1 in November, so he a year and a couple of months…"

"You know what I meant by that. Aye, you ain't gone believe it, but that's my name. John."

"You mean your name ain't Calvin no more? You done morphed into somebody else right in front of my eyes?"

"I can explain that. Let me explain a little better. That probably sounded crazy as hell."

"Yeah explain that please. You just sat here and told me your name Calvin. You trying to be funny or something?"

"I *go* by Calvin. My first name John. John Calvin. I just like to go by Calvin. Even my moms call me Calvin. I didn't know my dad so that's another reason why I rather not run around being called his name, you feel me? Umm when lil dude birthday? Just curious. November what?"

"It's November 17th. We had a little birthday party for him when she came for Thanksgiving. They stayed that whole week. She doing real good in Ohio."

Damn.

His name John just like that baby she turned up pregnant with. We all can put 2 and 2 together and get 4 honey. We ain't have no choice but do all that guessing. She didn't say *who* that baby belong to. As far as we knew that baby could belong to anybody but I can bet half my money – *half*, baby, just half of it, that Mr. Calvin is the other part of that baby. What are them odds that he happened to be lookin' around for a new shop? That's him honey. That man is the father of little John John. You watch and see what I tell you. She was already pregnant when Daddy brought her back here. I'm thinking that's the reason behind her wanting to clean herself up all of a sudden. She ain't foolin' *no* body. That child had been gone for a long while and then out the blue show up. Even let Daddy hisself of all sanctified come rescue her. And she of all of us know how *he* is. He probably *still* talking to her about it and she way in Ohio now. Naw child that had to be the main reason behind that decision. Once you tell him anything it ain't no going back the other way. If she had a thought that she wanted him to come pick her up, she wasn't gone be able to pick that phone up with no never-you-minds, honey. That was it and all to that one. She knew it too.

When she up and disappeared all of us was trying to find her. I don't know about everybody else but I knew she wasn't the most stable. Honey she was being held together with the high she was getting from them pills and whatever else she was on. She had enough money in the beginning to keep on getting high. Child she stayed high. Wouldn't listen to a damn piece of advice we had. I thought her signing herself off to that mental place was gone change something. It didn't at all baby, didn't change a thang.

The authorities ain't have no choice but to let that child go for that no good husband of her's murder. There was not one lick of evidence anyway honey not a speck. Other than her being so damn happy she could have went on ahead and used cartwheels to get herself from point A right to point B. Child she was so overwhelmed the man was out of her life and for forever that she thought she was crazy her own self. She was the one that checked into that crazy house. Now Daddy was just not having that. That girl was there long enough to eat a little bowl of tomato soup and a cheese sandwich for that dinner they served up and no more white jumper and buckles for her. He got her out of that place so fast in a hurry honey and let her know that she needed to get over it. Charles who, baby? He was not coming back anymore. Crazy…please, honey, Tawana wasn't no more crazy than she was sick of that man. She would never have to pay for what she did either. Not here on this earth.

I just knew that she was gone be a better person after escaping that fire honey. She had got another chance. Not many people would've been able to get out of something like that. I would've been on my best behavior personally. What about you? Not that one. Not that child. She kept on getting worse off. Good thing she did agree to take that big leave of absence from that hospital. That was what allowed her to keep that job of hers for as long as she did. During all that stuff going on honey there was no way she could've continued being sane. Had she been required to punch some time clock at that time, when all that was happening, honey, she would have been *un*employed. Bam. No more hospital. It would've taken a few days, not all them years to get that ax. We could have done something to help her. We family baby and ain't nothing like some good family in your corner. We the ones with your best interest in mind. Your family, honey. Tawana knows that good and well.

It do make a little sense sitting here putting it together. I'm just sitting here thinking about all of it. Baby a little sip of wine will have your wheels just a'turning! That or a hot bath. Too bad I can't take one of them right now since that man ain't got nothing on his agenda today. I guess I will be a little bit considerate for him. I don't want to wake him up. Then he will know it definitely ain't all about him, you know what I'm saying?

Anyway as it comes to me it may have been that environment why she came on back to us honey. I bet that's it. If that girl stayed on under whatever rock she was hiding under with the Lord only knows who, she probably would've self-destructed. She would've had the same access to them drugs she was taking right? That baby could have came to this world deformed or addicted to drugs too, who knows? And her first child too, honey. She did the right thing. It was better for her to go ahead and get away from that type influence. Daddy said it must've been a part of the plan. Who plan? Who plan Daddy? God's plan? Well, whoever had something to do with it - GOD or AHAYAH ASHER AHAYAH - it worked so somebody gets the glory. *Amen and Hallelujer* honey.

I personally would *not* have been jumping up leaving the man I was pregnant for 'cause baby if you helped to put it there it's your job to help me raise it. Kids expensive. A baby need its daddy to help you. And that man, my word! Ain't no worries for him. I was being paranoid all for no reason honey. Almost gave myself a heart attack thinking about who he could be sneaking up on us the way he did. There was not a clue about what he might've been up to. And then we find out we ain't have a thing to be worried about. I shoulda knew way better than that. He was never no kind of threat. Honey he was looking at that picture like he was in *mourning*. He was mourning that girl, baby, when he thought he was looking at a dead woman on that wall. He wasn't no mad at her for being too dead to collect some drug debt from. I felt so ashamed after I heard all that through that headset. I felt like some fool! I didn't even want to meet the poor guy after that ugly scene. Next time I will introduce myself to him, honey, and shake the man's hand even. And I don't shake no hands. I just might be shaking the hand of my future brother-in-law. We would have to make that happen wouldn't we? It just might be a possibility. Anything is a possibility I believe.

That's a sad thing honey 'cause I'm usually *real* good at judging characters. I have to be, with all the mass shootings and that gay bashing shit they do nowadays everywhere you look and on every news channel you turn it on. Just had several of 'em lately. Annalise Trego honey was one of my best friends in junior high school. She was my bestie. Child she had a heart of gold. This girl wasn't one of those girls that went out to party all the time and didn't drink no lot of alcohol either. If it was up to her she would rather sit at home and watch old episodes of What's Happening!! Or her favorite – Sanford and Son. That was her idea of a good night. It's a shame what happened to her because she wasn't even planning on going nowhere, honey, that sister of hers was the one out having the good time. Not even her.

Annalise was sitting there on her couch with that good-looking husband of hers after they had the kids all put down for the evening and ate their dinner baby, just enjoying each other. Then that phone rang for her. Jacky was one of them party animals, honey, in everybody's club every weekend. That girl needed a ride to their mama's house 'cause her friends had up and left her. That was her fault, she was in that bathroom baby with some man doing drugs, hooked on that coke. Anyway when Annalise went out to get her some shots was fired honey that was meant for somebody else out there standing on that sidewalk in front of that club that struck her. She died right there in front of that club waiting on Jacky to come on out of that bathroom. It wasn't over, baby. Because of that taking place the way it did on account of that phone call, that husband of hers killed little Miss Jacky. He shot her right at that funeral home. I guess he didn't see no reason for her to get to see her lying in state since it was her fault. He blamed her for calling Anna for that ride home.

That's the very reason I don't go NO place. I mean no bars and clubs, places like that. I'm no hermit, I am what you call selective I suppose. Anything could take place whether it was on purpose or just some kinda freak accident. Either way it just ain't worth it. You know it too. A good looking man walk in off the street and you so busy looking at how good he look to notice that he got a resting bitch face! Next thing you know the man done reached into his coat jacket and all your friends you picked up to have a good time at some club is laying dead at your feet! Then what you gone say? Whew, no no not me. I just don't care that much about snapping my fingers on no dance floor at no body's club. I can dance at home if I need to that damn bad.

People losing they lives at the gay bars all the time. I can't understand that. Why be so willing to shoot us all up because we happy with ourselves? Ain't our fault that you miserable. Whoever shooting everything up to pieces just not being honest with hisself or his family and them friends, you know? Some of them shootings may happen honey because that man mad he can't openly be hisself in his world. He mad. They all usually men. Women don't just walk in shooting. For what honey? It's always them men. That applies to the other prejudices too. Black churches and Jewish churches just as well. All of us getting shot at. It happen at the white churches, they ain't exempt. Crazy people in all races and religions. It's sad honey 'cause I still love my men with a passion. But by all accounts I have always been myself so I can admit something like that. Whatever makes *me* happy. My first priority is my own happiness. Me. Justin. I am ALL about myself first and foremost. Anyway child I got to be careful. I feel bad for how I overreacted, but they say it is better safe than laying somewhere sorry. That's the last thing I will ever be is sorry honey, ok? I need to keep all things considered you know what I'm talking about. I always got myself fully protected if you know what I mean along with Miss Cobi too. We took them classes. It's ok that we conceal what we carry. Hahaha. We got permission to hide our business baby.

When me and Daddy start talking again I need to make sure he know all about what happened with that Mr. John Calvin. Right now it's Daddy sending money to help her out with the baby. That girl ain't got no body else. That daycare by itself is expensive. Almost $200 a week for that KinderCare. Just so she can work at some gas station while she get herself back to how she was before. And that's one of those commercial centers. Richelle used to work at a KinderCare. We know all about them kinda centers honey. If she had him in somebody's living room or some ShaNeNe's Nest somewhere she wouldn't be paying all that money but that ain't no where near safe honey. I agree with her. That's better, baby, to have him in a place like that. You can't trust just no anybody with your babies.

That's me and Daddy's first conversation when he can get over me hurting them feelings of his. We got to talk about that man who could be that baby daddy. His money spend the same way, honey, while he helping her out with everything under that sun when he got a daddy walking 'round here.

It ain't nothing out of the extraordinary that Daddy mad at me. I am outspoken and it ain't new to him and no body else 'bout how I am. We spend more time than not going back and forth over that religion honey. Last time I talked to him he had nerve enough to say to me that I must be some kinda atheist because I don't believe what he preach about. That man told me I was lacking religion. I looked him square in his face and I asked him, Daddy what in the world are *you* talking about? I asked if he was aware of the fact that even if I *were* some atheist, which I am *NOT*, for his information, religion simply refers to a belief. That is *ANY* belief, honey, not just Christian belief or Catholic belief and in the second place the main issue was that picture that was hanging in that church. I told him that wasn't no Jesus picture hanging up there honey and I just didn't feel comfortable. What would be the reason for me coming to a church where the members can't even open a book to see who they worshipping? A *black* Jew baby don't look like nothing like that man with no silky straight hair. That picture all over the world of Jesus Christ is none other than Cesare Borgia in a *full* Roman toga. Leonardo Da Vinci painted that picture for all to look at. Look it up baby, Google. I guess they left that picture in place of those 14 books they stole right out the bible, that Apocrypha, so them nonreaders still don't know nothing, sitting there waiting on him to tell 'em. I sure declare honey, it is more than a notion. It wasn't nothing I told him that he couldn't see hisself if he was actually reading that 'Word' he carried along with him every step he took. I wanted to ask him if he actually opened it for anything other than as a prop when he was up in the pulpit 2-3 times every week but wasn't no point in doing that. Wasn't no way he could've been reading it.

Don't ever challenge that man about that bible honey, he will rip you up one side and down the other baby, but in my opinion just the same as I told him. Ain't no kinda challenge to take place if you don't even know the whole story. I call it when I see it, honey it's called acting. What him and the rest of 'em do every Sunday is nothing but 'pretend-play'. I flat-out refuse to go buy a whole wardrobe full of expensive clothes for that mess. Chile please.

What is the sense in getting all nice and dressed up with some beautiful hat on top of my head to go hear half of a story? Baby I need the *whole* story. Them sermons ain't even no where near related to nothing in that book no more than the money in them tithe envelopes is for that church. That's not for me honey you go right ahead. Running to that church house to hear some fable and pay tithes for the family is what you doing. Oh you didn't think about that did you baby? Oh yes ma'am. When we was little honey, them tithe envelopes paid Tawana's college tuition and was for that very ugly green Chevy Avalanche vehicle monthly due bill. Yes ma'am it sure was. Me go to church? Honey *please.*

I'm sitting up in this kitchen thinking 'bout all this stuff just going plumb crazy and in the meantime this man up there in the bed without a care in the world. Honey he is out cold. Make me wanna go pour a pot of water on him and wake him straight up. We got some talking to do about that mama of his living in that house over there like that. Honey her services are no longer needed so she is excused from being all in our business. The time has come for her to get some business all her own. She can go get a little apartment or some place. Child I am sick of that lady. I try to be nice and as courteous as I can be honey but the little patience I do have left is wearing very thin. Always keeping up a bunch of mess. She was Mama's aide honey when she got sick and she never did leave after she passed on away.

Daddy hired that woman. She came to help Mama out around that house when the both of us, me and Miss Cobi left there. Our lives had started, honey, we had life to live like going on college and doing hair. Miss Cobi had little Kennedy growing inside that belly honey. Two grown women can't live under no one roof so the one not paying the bills need her own house. Wasn't no body there except for Mama and her so honey I don't have one doubt they did get close, sure did, sitting up there talking and going on 'bout a lot of things. Being her friend didn't make her a part of no family. That is simply not how that happens!

She changed, that Catherine. I am not trying to say the woman wasn't nice, she was nice and all that. And respectful. She started running that mouth honey is what changed me in the other direction about her. Shoot she was living there with Mama so it ain't like we could show our true colors by any means. Me and my brother and sisters, honey, had to remain some type of way toward that woman. Mama didn't play that, honey even if we didn't care too much for her. *She* better not see it on our face and that was all to it. We was raised to respect our elders. Even if they was stone crazy.

That's how I met that man laying in my bed right this minute in the first place. Not that I need to like her for it, honey, but he was the only body coming through that door to see her since day one at Mama house. He was Catherine's baby boy. Me and him both the baby of the family. Honey that man is Catherine's youngest child. If not for him showing up to check on that Catherine honey, I wouldn't even know the man. I still can't stand that woman at all.

The man was fine, honey, sitting here thinking about that part of it. Not that he ain't right now 'cause if he was ugly he would not be in *this* house. Anyway I had no type of inkling at that time just how interested he really was, but honey that man started giving me them big goo-goo eyes. We ended up at the house together a lot of the time and we just started talking about a little of this and a little of that honey. After some conversation it was a little lunch down the way. A hamburger then on the next day a pizza. I just took to him just like that. He wasn't like Todd, oh no, honey, he was NOT trying to get fresh. He wouldn't even ask me for as much as a kiss so you know it wasn't none of that taking place at all, no baby. Not at all.

I got Mama's approval 'cause he was nice and respectful. And it was real. He wasn't puttin' on no kind of show because Elaine was my mother. Make no error, the way he was actin' around that house towards Mama and Catherine was genuine. You could tell that Catherine with all of her wickedness had given birth to him and he at the very least appreciated that. Honey I say that 'cause he was checking in on her regularly. If she needed anything he was there to hand it right to her. That mama of his was the first in his life. If she said jump he wanted to know how high honey. We all saw that. Mama saw exactly what was going on there. Five children that Cat gave birth to and fact of the matter is I got the best one out of all of them. I mean with all things considered.

Curtis was the only one out of all of them to even care anything about seeing that woman. I don't know if it was because he was the baby or what have you, but they had some kind of beautiful relationship between them. She was a pistol so I can't blame none of them other ones not one bit for keeping her at a far distance. All that talking she do, up in folk business. Oh yeah, baby, she was good at passing out them insults and putting her own kids down too. She useta call Lamille 'mousy' as if that was her own fault. I probably would have been quiet in nature too if my brother was raping me damn near my whole childhood. The boy didn't live with them because of all that bad behavior he was displaying. What he was doing may have been the way he expressed how he felt for his mama just giving him to that daddy of his. She couldn't handle him not another day honey. That is exactly what Curtis told me. His mannish ass was sitting up there raping his own baby sister like that.

When Lamille finally did tell that woman about that abuse it was many years after it went on. Child Lamille was a grown woman with a daughter her own self when Catherine found it out. Wasn't nothing she could do about that but blame Lamille for waiting so long to tell her. Never did even say a word about it to the man and honey that was something serious.

"Well girl why you just *now* talking 'bout it? Ain't you got no mouth? What am I supposed to do with that *now* this late in life? Wouldn't do no good to talk to him about that all these years later."

She called her own child mousy for not protecting herself. Her own mama. And for not telling somebody about it sooner. Couldn't nothing be done about it by the time she spoke up as far as she was concerned about what happened to her own daughter. That's what Curtis told me about it all. That jackass Charles was able to go on and live a regular life and get married. And with the type of past none of us knew about. Especially Daddy. That demon had a nice living off my sister and all along he was an evil spirit right under her roof. Poor sister of mine didn't know the first about it until she was already under lock and the key.

He took advantage too, baby, that my girl had it going on. She had a career honey and a little money from having a good family life. That was very unlike the one he had honey, living over there with that daddy of his. Baby he didn't even live in a house. Charles grew up in some low budget flat with the rats. Tawana always did own a house. We all was lucky honey. He reaped all those benefits when he got her to fall for him. The whole time he was over there treating her like some old dirty pig.

Daddy was angry about that whole situation honey. Especially after all that rape stuff came right on out into the open. Lamille waited until them two was hand-in-hand before she said something about him being a rapist on top of everything. Some friend she was. That could have been handled baby in a whole lot of other ways. If that was done the right way, honey, we wouldn't even know who that man was. Tawana would never know him to let him ruin her life the way he did. You see, baby, that Catherine is the cause for all that. That's what Daddy need to see. That woman is wicked. She even got the good preacher out of his character baby for the part he had to play in all that to save my sister.

Honey Tawana was so drunk she never saw Daddy in that backyard. That's his *daughter* baby. He was back there cleaning up that mess so the police wouldn't get her. As a matter of the facts honey, between me and you - it was Daddy who gave them authorities that confession. It was on a piece of stationary. The same type paper that used to be in Mama's purse. I know Mama didn't write no confession, honey, admitting she did a thing. That note went on and on about how she had to take that man out of here for the sake of her child. I didn't know what it was at first, up there on that dresser. Honey out of nowhere it came to me. Immediately. That chicken scratch was not Mama's signature. It was Catherine's. Yes ma'am Catherine wrote that confession.

Chapter 10: Jacobi's Man

He knew it was over between us, that we couldn't be together, but it wasn't over for him. He didn't have closure, he was telling me, the whole time hugging me and kissing me all over my face. I couldn't get out of arms, he was holding me so tight.

"I *love* you Jacobi. I don't want it to be over between us. I *love* you. Don't do this. Please don't do me like this."

"Do you like *what*?" I wanted to know. "We can't be together. You know we can't be together. It's bad enough that I'm pregnant. I can't be with you anymore. Especially because I *know* about you. Can you please just –?"

"Please *what*? Just let you go just like that? No. *NO.* I'm NOT leaving. We can work this out. You pregnant with our baby, Jacobi. That happened for a reason, baby, because we belong together."

"No. I don't know if I'm keeping the baby. I'm about to go back to school. I can't do this right now."

"You can't do that to me. To us. Don't talk like that. Please. She should be reason enough for us to be together. You can't just let this go like this. Don't you love me?"

"What you mean *she*? Boy you don't even know if it's a girl or a boy."

"It *is* a girl. I feel it. She wants her daddy to be with her mommy Jacobi."

He was rubbing my stomach, kissing my ear and telling me how much he loved me.

"I don't know -"

"You love me don't you?"

I wasn't about to answer that question. He knew I loved him. Loving him didn't have nothing to do with it. What did love have to do with anything? Love always broke hearts, didn't it? All because you can't help who you fall in love with this kind of shit always happened. It seemed like it was always happening to me. I could name a few people I called myself in love with. And that didn't matter in the end. I had to break away from him before it went any further than it had already. It was too toxic. We were spending all of our time together and then we started talking about getting married. He went out and bought me a diamond ring right after we started seeing each other. I was the fiancée and he was living in my house. Kennedy was calling him 'daddy'. It wasn't that he wasn't a good man. He was a good man, but there was no way to erase what I found out about him. It was better for both of us that we go our separate ways and leave it that way. To be honest it didn't matter too much because I was planning on leaving Georgia to go to school. I decided it was time for me to do something different with myself.

He didn't care what I was trying to tell him. His mind was already made up. He didn't hear a word I said. I could've told him the place was on fire and it went in one ear and out the other. I was getting weaker. He knew exactly what he was doing, trying to change my mind.

"Please. *Stop*. You have to go now. There's nothing to say."

"Can I? Please?"

He had slipped his hand in my pants and moved my panties to the side before he even asked that question. Oh my God it felt *good*! I watched him in the mirror on the wall and I was getting turned on by having him at full attention as he was concentrating on fighting a battle he had already won.

I had been horny for the whole 2 weeks we weren't together so I was definitely not hard to convince. He knew what I liked and he didn't waste any time getting right to the point. He was massaging my clit, rubbing it in circles between his fingers making it harder than it was from the moment he started kissing my ears. He knew that was my spot.

"For the last time?" He begged me. "Since it's over between us…I want to make you feel good. Please babe. One last time?"

I was already weak! His question had been answered without me having to say a word. He was licking his bottom lip looking the sexiest he ever had. It was obvious from the bulge protruding from the front of his joggers he wanted me. I could never resist him when he was like that. He made sure he got me to where I could literally cum even if he never pulled it out. We learned as soon as we made our first connection that we were a match made in heaven and we both had the power to turn each other on and off like a light switch. He was my weakness and I was totally onboard with whatever he wanted me to do.

He had only been there for 10 minutes and we were already on a pile of drying towels in the middle of the beauty shop floor, right next to where I saw the man getting his dick sucked up by Toine. I could see the bathroom where I found him from where I was laying, and could remember hearing him moaning, thinking I was going to catch him with some bitch. I thought about going to therapy because the man I loved was having sex with a man. I was thinking maybe it was me. Why would he want something like that when he had me? It bothered me so bad I didn't think I could ever have sex again, but I was wrong about that. What was happening at that very moment made me want to have sex. Too bad we couldn't be together. If not for him having his extra baggage to bring to the situation, or relationship, whatever you want to call it, we probably could have had a good life together.

When I met that man I thought I had found my soul mate; The person that was made especially for you. The perfect match. I heard people talk about soul mates all the time but it was bullshit to me because I had never met any man close to being a perfect match for me. Besides that I didn't need one. I thought I didn't need one until I met him. Every single thing about him was damn near perfect. I knew that shit was too good to be true.

This is our last time I bargained with myself, holding onto his ears and riding every stroke of his tongue, humping to my satisfaction so I could be in control of my orgasm. We could have a sexual relationship couldn't we? I changed my mind. It didn't have to be totally over between us I thought as I reached my climax and braced myself for his turn to feel what he had prepared for his turn to cum. We had a connection. A strong one. He made me feel like a queen and he was what I needed in my life after going through so many misfits. What was I going to do without him? I felt the same way he did and I was going to have to figure out a way to get over it. And then we had to convince everybody else to do the same thing.

We couldn't just act like it never happened. Not something like that. No matter how hard I tried to forget about it, it was always there. There was no way we could get married after finding all that out. I didn't see another option other than going our separate ways. There would be people hurt if we went through it and stayed together. What would people say about it? Especially me and him having a baby together. I didn't even want to think about that part of it. I just couldn't talk to him anymore and that was it. I would have to erase his numbers so I wouldn't be able to call him. My feelings were too deep for him to forget about him no matter what I did.

I couldn't thank Richelle enough for babysitting. I had to give her an extra $20 for keeping my baby for that long. I didn't get there until 10! I couldn't even bring myself to tell her why I was that late. I didn't need her judging me. Justin wasn't the only one I told about Toine's nasty ass. She knew about it too. I talked big shit about them being in that nasty shop instead of getting a damn room so you think I was about to tell my business? I wasn't in the mood to explain why I was in the shop having sex too. That wasn't none of her business. As far as she knew I was doing braids. She knew how long braids took. I did hers.

I was the one who helped Mike pay tuition for that school. $13,580.00! I wanted my money back. I had my own tuition to worry about. We didn't have to be in a relationship for me to get my money back. Him being a chef didn't help me. We weren't together. Why should he be making all that money working in that restaurant and not give me shit? If it wasn't for me he would be asking people what floor and asking to see identification in the government center. I did a lot for him. I bet he somewhere right now thinking he was the best thing that ever happened to me. That's how arrogant he was.

I'm sure he was waiting for me to call him to come back. He would see how much I needed him. I was about to move on *without* him and I was still going to wear his ring. I could hear Justin now saying 'A diamond is a diamond baby it don't matter why it's shining!' I wanted everybody who didn't know me to think I had a husband to go along with my big old belly. The school I applied to wasn't some community college. I would be surprised if I got there and there was another black girl like me there. Not only am I a young black girl, but by then if I decided to keep the baby, I would be about 5 or 6 months pregnant too. I didn't need to broadcast the fact that I was another young girl having babies with no husband. I needed that ring. That was the least he could do to support us since he wasn't going to be around.

Justin would know exactly how to handle this. He was always good with coming up with the right thing to do about everything. It always came natural to him other than that time Cassie came over our house about Todd and their baby. Having Justin for a brother was better than having a best friend. As a matter of fact that's why I never had a best friend. I had my brother. It seemed a little strange not talking to him, but me and his relationship as brother and sister was over with and as buried as Charles was. We weren't teenagers liking the same boy! We were adults. How could my brother betray me like he did? He knew Mike was cheating on me and didn't even bother to tell me. And I'm his damn sister. Here I was about to marry Mike like a dummy and Justin knew the whole time that he was fucking that boy behind my back. I don't care about him denying it because for a fact him and Toine talked about sex and who he had sex with just as much as they talked about what they were having for lunch. He could've at least told me what was going on instead of making a fool out of me by not saying shit about it. It made my stomach turn knowing how many dicks Toine kept in his mouth and then to find out Mike's was one of them.

Maybe if it wasn't Antoine he was getting off with I could have at least tried to forgive his lying ass. It was harder for me to accept who it was who basically took my man from me like that. And what I really couldn't understand was why he was willing to risk what we had for some ugly ass dude. That was so embarrassing. Jay fired him after all that happened, but it wasn't right away. I still had to go up in there every day and look at him! That made me even *more* mad at Justin for not having my back. I used to always have his back all the time. Up until all this came out. Even after he started messing around with Todd's ass I stood up for him. People was out there calling him names and saying he was confused and all that. I told him he better not ever take another boy away from me or I would get him back, but I didn't let that come between us. I hold it against him now though. 'Cause I see how he really is. I see his true colors. I ain't gone never trust him again. I'm done with Jay.

Richelle told me she heard Toine didn't even get fired for what he did to me. It was for stealing customers. I guess he was doing heads at his house for half what they paid at the shop. Jay wasn't having that. Money was before loyalty to him. Had he not stole customers, he would still have a job there like nothing ever happened. I didn't want the whole shop in my business but I couldn't help it. I told him if I ever found out he was with Mike after that I was going to kill him on general principle, on GP! Whether we was together or not.

"Bitch if you *ever* touch him again I will slit your fuckin' throat and say it was a hate crime when they ask me about you." I let him know.

"I can't *believe* you said a thing like that girl. I told you I was sorry. Threatening me like that! That kind've talk ain't nothing to be playin' wit Miss Cobi."

"Oh no no bitch, that's a promise not a threat. I *hate* hoes like you, up in my face, but sucking my man's dick behind my back. It *would* be a HATE crime. Trust me. And I would *LOVE* to do it bitch!"

Justin had the nerve to say I needed to be mad at Mike and not Antoine. What the fuck? Where has he been this whole time? He saw that boy in my face every day. Constantly going downstairs to get both of us coffee! Antoine was the one who helped me plan that birthday party at the Mirage as a matter of fact. I should've reminded Jay of *that* shit! How was he saying I was the one wrong for confronting that backstabbing ass boy? Jay just needed a reason to distance himself from the situation so he didn't have to take sides. I'm done with having him as my brother. I was turning my client around to face a different way when he was up there doing a head. Love hurts remember? Love always ends up breaking your heart. Mine is still broke.

Always sitting at that computer typing up the Truth, he called it, as usual. The last time I went over his house I was mad at him, but he was sitting there lookin' all cute typing his ass off with them nails all shiny. He looked like a real author, wearing his red and white polka dot shirt with his Michael Kors sandals and a denim crop pants on. I did miss that about him. I don't know why I did it, but I took a picture of him. I wasn't planning on ever running into him again. I wasn't coming back when school started. I was going to make my life somewhere else just like Tawana did. If anybody wanted to see me and my kids they could come to South Carolina.

If it were any other time I would've been right on the internet trying to find me a bright color polka dot shirt and some denim crop pants to go with it but fuck Jay. I wasn't copying shit he had on. I looked at it like it was his fault I was in my predicament. If it wasn't for me being mad at his ass I wouldn't be thinking about going to school to get the hell out of that shop. Probably wouldn't even be pregnant either.

I don't know how he got into tearing the bible apart like that. He was sitting in church next to me his whole life and getting dragged over Daddy's house every Sunday just like I was. Now he talkin' about God's name ain't Jesus because the scribes added stuff to the bible. Saying there wasn't no letter j back then, so his name wasn't Jesus. How he know all that? I don't want to hear all that. That's scary. It sounds like a bunch of bullshit just to start stuff. It do be starting stuff. When you start telling people all that, it's like they start noticing it for real. They start wondering if it is true. They call it 'waking up' Jay said. He said he was gone be the one to wake them all up. I don't know how he was gone do all that. Wasn't no body trying to read nothing about that! I don't know what he can't understand about people not wanting to deal with change. Not with no religion!

Him and Daddy argued all the fucking time about their beliefs. I didn't see why it mattered. Jay could believe in whatever he wanted to, that didn't mean he had to throw it in everybody else's face. Whenever Daddy came to the shop to get his little afro lined up, there they go arguing. Going back and forth about what Daddy was preaching about and then whenever I talked to Daddy that was our whole conversation as if I wanted to talk about Justin. Fuck Justin. Talking about he didn't want him to go to hell. How the fuck did he know if what he was talking about was bond? He didn't have all the goddamn answers. I don't know why he thought he was the one right insteada Daddy.

This knowledge has been hidden but the Most High said in the last days, knowledge would increase. (Daniel 12:4). The Most High people would begin to wake up to who they are and wake up to everything going on around them. This knowledge is important in our learning because if we can't identify ourselves

in the Bible, how can we be so sure that our pastors/preachers and teachers are giving us the correct information and even how can we be sure that they were given the correct information? You are responsible for your own soul salvation. How do we know that we are following the word of the Most High? Revelations 12:9 says Satan deceives the whole world.

The Georgia Gazette! Biggest pastor in Georgia and his own son putting stuff like this out there. I can't believe him. Was he forgetting he was *gay*? What would Daddy do if Jay sent this kind of stuff to the church? Probably cut him off. Maybe that's what needed to happen since Jay likes to run around hurting people. He needs to see how it feel to be hurt. He probably wouldn't even miss the pamphlets I took he had so many.

Chapter 11: New Life

When I got pregnant with John John I knew I had to change somehow. I didn't know how I was going to kick the habit, but I wanted to at least try. If I didn't I was going to kill both of us. I had it bad. I was addicted to anything that could alter my mood and heroin did it best. It relaxed me so much I didn't have any problems when I used it. It was like being in a dream. I felt peaceful. I was walking around with my head in the clouds during those times instead of being all depressed thinking about Mommy dying and what I did to Charles even though I hated him with all of my heart.

I had a conscience at the end of the day. I couldn't live with myself knowing that I was a murderer. I used to be so calm when I got high that it wouldn't have fazed me if anything happened no matter what it was. My heart would've beat the same rhythm no matter what was going on. I didn't feel pain, remorse or fear. During those times I never thought about Mommy or Charles, that's just what it did to me. It became my own personal therapy.

My whole world revolved around getting high. Being pregnant and having Calvin in my life should have been the most important thing in the world to me but even the thought of having a family again – my own family - meant nothing. The day I took that pregnancy test and found out I was having the love of my life's baby do you know how I celebrated? I celebrated by shooting up. Here I find out I am finally pregnant and instead of eating healthy and giving all that up I was shooting heroin into my placenta. I even missed my first prenatal appointment. I knew how important it was to find out what kind of harm I had already done to my baby, but I didn't want them to know I was on drugs! As soon as they drew the prenatal labs they would see that and I didn't want them trying to take my baby. I had plenty of time to get myself together. I decided I would go then.

I never thought I would ever be somebody's mother anyway. I remember trying to convince myself that the test was wrong. It had to be wrong because I wasn't ready for something like that. I saw babies born messed up all the time at the hospital. Those babies were born addicted to heroin and all small. They had tubes in them and cried all the time. Why would God deal me a hand like that? That's a big responsibility to be responsible for another person and I couldn't even take care of myself, out doing drugs and killing myself when I knew I shouldn't have been. And I couldn't stop even knowing it could kill me. How could I out of all people be pregnant? The only time I cared about being pregnant in the first place was when I was sober. When I was sober my focus was still more on getting high again than it was wondering how little John John was doing in there.

It took a while, but I started waking up. I kept seeing all the deaths from overdosing. It was always somebody in the obituaries dead from it. It always said something like how so-and-so lost their 6 year battle with heroin or 8 year battle with addiction, but went on to say how full of life they were or how they were so passionate about whatever job they had. That didn't make sense to me. *I* wasn't full of life. I felt like I was drained of life. I could stand back and look at myself as if I was another person and see the dead Tawana standing there. I was killing myself and couldn't stop. If I didn't get help I would be dead at the age of 36 and my child would never have a chance to live.

Calvin would have done everything he could to help me if I gave him the chance. I know he cared about me. He asked me all the time to get help so we could move forward. He offered to go with me and asked me if I wanted him to find my family so they could help me. He actually believed me when I told him I didn't know where my family was. They weren't the ones hiding. They were in the same place they had always been. I was the one lost not them.

I used to be so *mean* to him. I didn't want his help! I was mad at him for even trying to help me. What made him think I wanted to get off drugs? I liked the feeling of being high did that thought ever cross his mind? After a while he didn't mention it anymore. We stopped talking about it. I guess he was sick of getting his head bit off.

"You will let me help you when you get ready," He used to say to me all the time. He really believed that. He didn't know nothing about drugs because he never had the problem. Smoking weed wasn't the same thing. Heroin was different. Weed was a recreational drug not something you would rob and damn near kill somebody to get. That's where I was. There was no way he could ever understand that. All he saw was the same old Tawana he met a long time ago at the pool. I didn't look the same and I wasn't the same person he met either. Even my body was different. Being in love with a person is looking past faults, but I know he noticed all the changes. And it was getting worse. I was a drug addict, not blind. I could see how I looked like death was standing on my front porch. Calvin acted like he couldn't see the abscesses all over my face and how my hair was all matted. He still kissed me the same as he always had like he didn't even care about who I had become. I sold my stuff and his stuff too if he didn't lock it up in his car or at work I found out later. He still never did judge me for none of it.

I wanted to tell him. I wanted to tell him I was pregnant and I needed help but he would want me to stay and there's no way I could stay there. The dealers didn't mind giving me credit around there. They knew Calvin got a check every 2 weeks. That's what I told all of them. They knew that whatever they gave me Calvin was going to take care of it. That wasn't fair to him. Especially knowing that he was doing it because he was in love with me. Anything I wanted I could get from him because he wanted to spend the rest of his life with me and I found myself taking advantage of it. I was to him what Charles was to me and I wanted to change that. I loved him. I wanted to spend the rest of my life with him too. The only way I was going to be able to do that was to leave. If I didn't I was going to die. Me and the baby.

The old me would have never fathomed anything like this, living the way I was having to be basically rescued from my own self. I had turned into the person I used to feel sorry for: Weak and hooked on drugs. A drug addict with nothing going on. Nothing at all. I used to always wonder how people managed to get like that. For a high that didn't last long. Spending any dollar you could find on getting high. Blowing the rent money, losing the roof over your head. That was who I had become. I didn't want to be that person any more. I had to call my daddy. I didn't even know what to say to him. My own father. I didn't have any explanations. I couldn't explain why he hadn't seen me in almost 3 years. I didn't have to. He just asked me where I was so he could come and get me. He already knew. He always knew.

I didn't leave a note when I left that Sunday. The urges just kept coming and I couldn't wait around anymore trying to do it myself. Daddy was the last person I wanted to see me like that. A drug fiend. Feeling like I needed them or I would die. I saw a treatment place online called Meadowview Treatment Facility. I was reading the reviews for it and it was supposed to be one of the best ones for heroin addicts specifically. I wanted to go - I had to go.

I took a handful of tithe envelopes out of his drawer. It was like $4000.00 I think. More than enough to get me to Ohio. The fact that I didn't know anybody there was even better. I didn't have anything to lose. I had already lost everything except the baby growing inside of me. Me and Calvin's baby. It was all about saving me from myself.

I wanted to be normal. Normal meaning family dinners and being around each other. After being by myself like that, living like a psycho for so many years I couldn't wait for the day I could be with my brothers and sister – their kids – mine. Back when Mommy wasn't sick and Jason lived with us in Georgia we used to go out for ice cream and on holidays we rented movies and sat around eating like pigs. We used to talk about anything and everything. We just had fun. Together. I missed that. I missed Jay and all his stories and Cobi's crazy ass putting people's stuff out of her house.

I wanted to hug my daddy more than anything. Calvin deserved an explanation too. The way I left him was wrong. I wanted to tell him that I left for *us*. To make our relationship better. I had to get off drugs.

'Hi Daddy!"

"Hey baby! I was wondering when I would get to hear your voice again!"

"I know. I'm sorry Daddy – I've been kind of busy lately! I've been thinking about you though," I assured him

"And I always think about you – all those cities away from me. You know I'm in the habit of talking to you at least once a week now. I like to hear your voice at least since I can't spend any time with you.''

"I can't wait to see my grandson," He told me. "I know he's a big boy now. Last time I layed my eyes on him, it was Thanksgiving. Almost two whole years ago. When you coming home for a visit to see your family? We sure do miss you."

"Daddy we will be there as soon as I get this house together! You know how it is when you get a new place! I'm STILL unpacking stuff around here. There's so much stuff to do."

Daddy had insisted on sending money every month like clockwork when I got out of rehab. I had to get a P.O. Box because I didn't have no place to go. I was renting a room at a motel. I definitely didn't want him to know that. He would've really been trying to take me back to Georgia.

"There's no locks on the mailboxes at this complex Daddy," I lied. "Can you send it to my P.O. Box?"

"Sure Honey. Anything you say," He believed me. "Is that all I can help you with?"

I wanted to tell him no, but I was feeling like a real failure at that point. I had some money left so I went to one of those buy-here-pay-here places and got a minivan. We had to sleep in the van for awhile. It was better than sleeping on the street! I had to think that way because it wasn't just me any more. I was somebody's mother.

I didn't want to ask him to help me get a house since I owed him all that money, but I didn't have no room for pride. I was paying $200 a month for that van and the room was $69 a day. I wasn't getting anywhere. And my baby deserved a decent place to live. Daddy never mentioned the money even though I know he noticed it. And I was going to pay him back every penny. I didn't have no choice. I had to ask him. If he knew how I was living he probably would've been mad at me for *not*.

"Daddy? I need to move," I started.

I want to say I was signing on a new house exactly 30 days after I asked him.

"I been thinking about some stuff and I want to get your opinion. I don't want you to be late getting to the church though so I'm gonna call you later on tonight."

"No, it's quite alright," He interrupted. "I'm not going today."

"*You*? Miss *Bible* Study? Are you sick? Is everything ok?"

"Well I can't really say. I honestly don't know. It's been going on now for some time and I don't know what to make of it. The church is not the same anymore. Not too many members show. You remember now, was so packed on Sundays it used to be standing room only. Bible Studies were like – they were like church services with all the classrooms filled. Had different sessions going at the same time."

"I remember that. Y'all used to drag me to Bible Study too. Everybody who came to church went to Bible Study on Wednesdays."

"Not any more. Those times I'm afraid, have been long gone."

"What happened Daddy? Why? I don't understand that. Do you ask about it on Sundays? You had over 300 members in that church. NO body shows up?"

"Maybe 2, 3. Mother Jackson conducts the study for those Mothers since she sits on the board with them. Just as well. Gives me a chance to catch up on my reading."

"Wow Daddy. That's not good. I would be trying to get to the bottom of it. Something must've happened."

"I'm sure I will in due time. What did you want to talk about? I am all ears."

"I wanted to talk to you about Calvin - "

"Jacobi's boyfriend? How do you know him?"

"Jacobi got a boyfriend named *Calvin*? That's a coincidence. But naw, I'm talking about John John's daddy. His real name is John."

"Ok. Well what about this John? He there with you?"

"No that's just it. I want him to be. He don't know about the baby. Remember you came downtown and got me before I left? I was leaving him. Well not leaving *him* per se, but the situation. To get better. It was *for* him. So we could be a family. He didn't even know about the baby."

"You thinking you want to find him is that it? Let him know he's got a handsome son and show him how good you're doing? Maybe you can eventually pick up things where you left off."

"Well… yeah. That's what I want to do. Not just for me. John John too. He needs him. And he was always a good man to me. I know he would be a great dad to him. Especially when he finally gets to me him. He always wanted a son. A junior."

"Did you try to find out where he's at yet? Still here in Georgia?"

"Not yet 'cause I was waiting for the right time. I hope I can find him. It has been a long time. I hope he didn't move out of town like I did."

"All you need to do nowadays is type his name in and it'll pop up somewhere. Where ever that is. His address and such."

"Yeah I didn't even think about doing that. Can you look it up for me? I don't have wifi yet. That would be a good start, if I could find out where he at from the internet."

"Marshall, right? Calvin Marshall?"

"Look up John. John Marshall or John C. Marshall."

"I see now. Calvin is a middle name. Alright let me see. John Calvin Marshall. Looks a lot like my grandson from this here mugshot Tawana…at age 19, and now it seems he lives on – Craigwood."

"What? What else does it say? Why did you stop talking?! He's not dead is he? You see an obituary or something? What is it?"

"This is strange. He lives at 3246 Craigwood Drive."

"What does THAT mean? That new suburb over there in the Hills? You think he came into some money or something?"

"No it's not that. Craigwood Drive is Jacobi's street. That's *her* house number listed there."

"Wait a minute… So in other words Cobi's boyfriend is John? *John John's* daddy?"

"Let's not jump to conclusions – "

"You SAID Jacobi's boyfriend when I said Calvin Daddy. So that's gotta be the case. It's right there. He lives with her."

"I will get down to the bottom of it. I'm sure she could NOT have known about this. I can't see her doing such a thing, Tawana, I just can't. Her own flesh and blood sister? As soon as she comes through that door - and I mean the very minute she opens that door - I will get down to the bottom of it."

"She on her way over there? I need to talk to her ass. She just a hoe. All the men in Georgia and she gone just mess around with the only one I wanted? It ain't fair. I wanna know if she knew."

"Now Tawana calm down. I told you I will try to get to the bottom of it and I will."

"Maybe *that's* what she coming to tell you, thinking she can make it seem like she didn't know. Especially since she pregnant. That girl from the shop told me she pregnant. You know Tyrone's sister Richelle. That's who she hang with. *She* was the one who told me Jacobi was pregnant. It probably ain't even *by* Mike. Trying to tell you first."

"I actually don't think that was the motive Honey. She told me she was going through something with Justin again - I didn't pay much attention to what it was. I'm guessing she feels I need to know about whatever it is this time."

"I'm on my way Daddy, I need to talk to her myself."

Chapter 12: Turning Point

"Oh my God! I'm glad you here! He still in surgery. Everybody here."

"What *happened* Curtis? Is he going to make it or –"

"They said it's a brain injury. That's all they told us. They rushed him right to the operating room so we don't know nothing yet. It don't look good baby."

"Brain injury? What happened? How did he get a *brain* injury? That's serious."

"They was down there arguing. Then they started fighting child. I don't know. It woke me up out of my sleep."

"Who was fighting?"

"Jay and your daddy honey. They got to fighting."

"My *daddy*?"

"Yeah. Jay was crying. He told him he was sorry, that he didn't mean for all that to happen like that, but it was too late I guess. Girl your daddy was calling him every name under the sun. I ain't never heard him talk like that. He was dropping F-bombs and I don't know how many 'punk mothafuckas' he called him. By the time I got down them stairs he was hitting him over and over again."

"Who? Jay was hitting my daddy?"

"Naw, honey, your *daddy* was beating up on *Jay*. That's what I seen. It was happening so quick all I saw was Jay fall over that…the ottoman or whatever. I saw it. I saw him do it, Hit him in the back of the head with that statue."

"A statue? My daddy hit him with a statue?"

"After Jay said he was a fake-ass preacher stealin' folk money, Mitchell picked that statue up and BAM! Hit him. Knocked him straight down."

"I can't believe that. My daddy not like that. I wonder what money he was talking about? Jay ain't got no dealings with Daddy's money. And he don't go to church. Or over his house."

"That was my first time hearing about it. He just kept saying it was Jay fault he lost all that money. That's all I know. He didn't say nothing else. All I know is I ain't *never* seen him like that. That man wasn't the same one that be up there in that pulpit."

"Did Jay say anything?"

"Just that he didn't mean for all that to happen. That was all he said. That was all he could say honey. Your daddy wasn't trying to hear a thang he had to say."

"I know they ain't never got along, but that's because Jay don't believe the same stuff Daddy preach about. That been going on for years though. That ain't nothing new for them to start fighting about now. That's why this ain't making no sense. Jay ain't got nothing to do with Daddy's money so what was he talking about? Jay make all that money at the shop. He got his own money."

"I don't know. I'm just as confused as you honey. All I know is he was breathing fire about whatever it was. Told Jay he wasn't none of his son. I thought he was about to kill him. I couldn't find not a one of them cell phones to call the ambulampse to help him, I was so busy begging your daddy to stop kicking him. I went into shock. All the blood on that white carpet I thought he was laying there *dead*. I didn't even realize I had my damn phone in my hand."

"Damn. His *head*? His head was bleeding like *that*?"

"Yeah it was bleeding pretty bad. He hit him hard with that statue."

"Did Daddy try to help him at all? After he saw him bleeding like that?"

"Naw, believe it or not he was still yelling at the man. My body just went weak. I was trying to let that operator know what was going on and at the same time begging your daddy to look at what he did and help me get him up. I didn't know what to do Tawana. I was having some out-of-body experience at that point. It was almost like he didn't know he had knocked him out."

"How was he acting when you were on the phone with 9-1-1? Did he look like he was sorry for hurting him like that?"

"Nope. He just turned around and walked on out the door. Slammed it shut behind him."

"It's sad. I wonder do anybody know where he is. Did somebody see if he was at the church? That might be where he went."

"I don't know. I don't have a clue where he coulda went when that door slammed after him. I been here with my baby, honey, he the one who needs us. Not your daddy. That's what's important now. We don't even know how Jay is gone make it through all this. Your daddy'll turn up somewhere. Especially when it hit him."

"Yeah you right. 'Cause I know he didn't mean for this to happen. They have their differences, but he raised him. When Jacob died my daddy took over for him. That's his son no matter what. I don't care if they got along or not. How long he been back there? I wonder how long the surgery take?"

"They didn't say. It was an emergency surgery. They was taking him back there to the operating table as soon as the ambulampse pulled him in here. I am scared to death that is for sure. I don't feel like this is really happening. I ain't never been this scared in my life. I need some coffee or some tea or something. I'm about to lose my mind up in here girl. My entire mind, ok?"

"It don't *ever* stop. It's *always* some drama going on in my family."

"I just hope he makes it through this. He can't die. I couldn't handle that at all. I think I would just die myself if something happened to him."

"That would *kill* me."

"It would kill me too. This kind've stuff don't happen other than in the movies."

"We can't be thinking like this. What would Jay say if it was the other way around? Jay is going to be ok. I prayed about this honey. I prayed to the Most High that my baby was going to be just fine."

"Did you call anybody else?"

"Naw, chile, I dialed the first number I got to. Yours. I was too out of it to dial up anybody else and explain it all over again. That Jacobi changed her phone number and I was gone let you call up Jason. I was too busy trying to make sure he was ok the whole ride here."

"Jason? Justin is having emergency surgery, I told him. "I don't want to scare you, but I think it would be a good idea if you get here as soon as you can. I just got here myself so I don't know. I guess him and Daddy got into it pretty bad and he – She did WHAT? Are you SERIOUS? Oh my GOD Jason!"

"What he sayin' girl? What is it?"

"Ok Jason I'll be here. I'm not leaving this hospital. No I don't have to worry about it, he stayed in Columbus at Karen and Larry's. He was playing with Cassie's twins. Ok. We at Mt. Caramel. Bye."

"What he say?"

"He just told me Jacobi did all this."

"Jacobi?"

"Apparently she told my Daddy it was Justin fault everybody stopped going to the church. Jason said he had just called Daddy to ask him about something and Daddy told him he had to call him back because he was on his way to y'all's house. He said Jacobi told him what Justin did. I guess she was laughing about it."

"That's because she was lying. Laughing though? She is so miserable, I can tell you that. Ruining people's lives like that."

"Let me call this miserable *bitch*. Got my brother back there about to die for doing same shit she does to people. Our kids got the same daddy and we sisters, but she mad Justin didn't tell her about her gay-ass boyfriend? Where they do that at?"

"Hello?"

"Bitch where is you at?"

"Tawana I ain't in no kinda mood to start arguing with you."

"You need to get up here to Mt. Caramel. Justin in surgery."

"Surgery? What kind of surgery? Why is he in surgery?"

"Him and Daddy got in a fight because of you lying on him."

"Lying on him? Lying about *what*?"

"Sending them letters out. Justin didn't do that. YOU did it. "

"What kind of letters?"

"There you go, with your simple ass. Trying to play dumb. You know what you did. You told Daddy it was Justin fault he ain't have no more members. It wasn't Justin who did that and you know it. Now Justin back there going through it for nothing. He would never in a million years do something like that to Daddy."

"I know he put that Truth or whatever he call it in the Georgia Gazette. Daddy's members probably saw it. You know how he started off talking about that wasn't really Jesus in the pictures, it was some man named Cesar…"

"You just said he put it in the Gazette? That's his damn opinion. He can put whatever he wants to in the paper, on a billboard, WHEREVER. What that got to do with my Daddy? He didn't send shit to the church. He put it in the paper. You was the one who sent the letters to people."

"I forgot the last name of the man in the pictures, but he was always talking about Pagen holidays and …"

"Girl who cares about all that? What the fuck did you do? You can't even keep your story straight for real. You mad Jay ain't tell you about your gay-ass man and blaming him for it."

"I wasn't mad about him being gay. Toine was HIS fuckin' friend. He knew about it, saying he didn't! That pissed me off! Ok yeah. I DID copy that shit and I sent it out to everybody in that church."

"If my brother dies *BITCH* his blood is on *your* hands."

"I didn't want all this to go down! I wasn't trying to hurt him. All I wanted was for Daddy to cut his ass off. Take that fuckin' building from him."

"Why? Why would he deserve all of that Jacobi? Over Mike?"

"Naw not for Mike. It's not about Mike. For stabbing people in their back. Stabbing *FAMILY* in the back."

"Oh you mean how you fucked my man and had a daughter with him? Is that the kind of stabbing family in the back you're talking about? You know, bitch – my brother got his head busted open because of some shit you did. How about this? How about you and your new husband Calvin come see about him. Sorry-ass hoe."

"Doctor is he alright? How is he doing? I'm his sister."

"We did everything we could - "

"What are you saying Doctor?"

"He didn't make it? Justin *died*?"

"I am truly sorry. There is no easy way to say this. There was too much damage done. We did everything we could. Again I am sorry for your loss. Excuse me."

Chapter 13: Weep What You Sow

"Over here!" Sharon was waving.

"Oh my God! There they are! Look at her! She looks absolutely beautiful!"

"Hi baby!" I kissed her cheek. I missed you all so *much*. Look at my family! How are you doing Sharon? Aren't *you* a sight for sore eyes, like Mommy used to say! Hey boys. It's been a long time since I've seen the two of you."

"Hi Auntie."

"Hi Aunt Jacobi, you look nice today."

"How long has it been *this* time?"

"Quite some time. But at least this time it's *good* news and not bad."

"Yeah I know. I hear you. It started to seem like we only got together for funerals. And where is that little Micah? Already turning 6-years-old! I can't believe it! I wanna meet her. All I get to see are pictures. I know Kennedy has her hands full with that little diva. She was an only child for a long time and then Micah came along. Where are my nieces anyway?"

"In the lobby getting something to drink. That little diva is *always* thirsty. She drinks like a fish! Tawana! Oh my goodness, you made it!"

She had a big gift bag that had 'CONGRATULATIONS' across the front of it. The fact that she even came was the gift as far as I was concerned. Especially after what I did to her. It had been almost 7 years since Justin's funeral. I sent text messages and emails to her all the time hoping she would respond one day. She never did until now. Showing up to my graduation. I sent an invitation to her and Daddy. He didn't totally ignore me. Half answers are better than none at all I figured.

"I couldn't miss your graduation girl! You are still my sister aren't you? Miss Nurse Practitioner. Daddy here too."

"He is?! Where he at?"

"Over there getting programs. You know he keeps all that stuff in that album. He still has mine from Preschool believe it or not. Here he comes."

Daddy hugged me so tight I thought I was going to break in two!

"Daddy you told me you were sick!

"I guess I pulled the wool over *your* eyes then Sweetheart."

I couldn't stop smiling.

"I was looking forward to seeing John John. Too bad he couldn't have come with you Tawana."

"Yeah I know. Maybe next time. He'll get a chance to meet his *Uncle* Calvin eventually. You haven't met his new dad yet. My husband Bryson adopted him right after we got married. He's all he's ever known. Couldn't have found a better father for him"

"That's awesome. I'm so happy for you Tawana."

"Kennedy! Oh my goodness! My precious Kennedy! And this must be – Micah? Hey girls!"

"Granddad! My aunt! Daddy look! It's Aunt Tawana! Micah, this is our aunt! I missed you so much Aunt Tawana! Guess what!

Mommy is graduating! She finished school! She's going to be a Practitioner...A *Nurse* Practitioner!"

"I know! I had to come see her graduate. I'm proud of her too!"

"Hello Mr. Mitchell."

"Calvin. How are you?" Daddy asked him. "Hi girls!"

"Nice to see you."

"Yeah you too Calvin. Good to see you too."

"Oh, I gotta get up there. It's starting!" I let them know.

"CONGRATULATIONS GRADUATES!!! He called out to all of the graduates seated in the first 20 rows. There is so much to be thankful for today! Today is one of the most meaningful and momentous milestones for you and your families. You are finally ready to embark on the next endeavor..."

The speech was perfect. Jason did a great job up there. He was our commencement speaker. I don't know how he did it. He didn't mess up once! He was a natural.

"You will find yourselves doing everything by the book, writing in the charts and that's perfectly normal in the beginning. One you are comfortable you will find you have scribbled those same notes on your lunch napkin or the back of your hand...hahaha! It's fine, don't worry. It means you are comfortable with what you're doing. Be confident!" He told us.

Right after Jason gives his speech everybody's clapping and crying. The stage looks like a field of daisies with all the yellow caps and gowns. All those years of blood, sweat, and tears. Up for hours every night studying is over! We all made it. Every one of us. I was sitting next to all of the girls who were in my classes. We had been in many a study group trying to take all that information in so it would be like a second nature to us when we would have actual patients who depended on us.

I move my tassel to the other side at the very end of the ceremony. That's when Justin comes out of nowhere and pulls out a knife. I try to fight, but it's too late. He towers over me, blaming me for his life being cut so short. Stabbing me over and over again until I can't move anymore. I can't move, but I can feel every single stab. Blood is everywhere, all over my gown, all over the stage – Tawana is screaming for him to stop, but he won't listen to her. His focus is on me, wanting me to just die, but my eyes are still open. Watching him. It always wakes me up every time! Me jumping up like that always wakes Calvin up.

"That same nightmare?"

"The one about Justin killing me. Yeah."

"Awww, you always safe with me, my lady, believe that."

"Yeah, I know I am. I think its meeting your family that has me all nervous like this."

"Why is that? They cool people. I talk to some of my cousins in Chicago. They real cool."

"It just seems like every time I get nervous or anxious about something I start having those nightmares, that's all. Plus I been thinking about Justin and my Daddy lately too. His birthday is coming up and I used to look forward to that. He used to have these festivals for his birthday. We used to have to plan those months in advance. He would've been turning 39 this year. He been dead about 6 years now. Almost 7."

He just listened. That was one of the things I loved about Calvin. He was a listener. He wasn't the type of person to interrupt you when you was talking or none of that. I was glad to have somebody there for me. Everybody else had turned their backs on me. I didn't blame them for it I just missed them a whole hell of a lot. I couldn't even get mad when they released Daddy's body to Tawana and they had the services without even letting me know about it. It was at Greater St Mary's too. He wouldn't have had it any other way. The building had been closed for years, but when he died, she had it opened back up for his services. That's what he would've wanted. At least he was able to go home in style after living in that prison cell for all them years. I hate to say it, but at least he wasn't there for the 20 years they gave him for killing Justin.

I had destroyed my entire family starting with me and Calvin messing around. Then it was Justin and Daddy. I ain't have no choice but leave Georgia. I was too ashamed to stay there. After doing all that I had to go. I didn't mean for that to happen to Justin. Or to Daddy. I was just that mad and wasn't even thinking about the whole thing. Like what would happen for real. After Tawana told me he had died I just started packing. I went to Wal-Mart and bought about 30 totes. Like she said I had blood all over my hands so I was running. Running from the shit I did my own self.

When Calvin came home the whole living room was filled with totes. He just saw me packing and started packing right along with me. We packed up the closets and drawers, the kids room, we packed up the kitchen. Everything. Anything we could pick up was going in a tote. He didn't bother to ask what was going on because he already knew. The last text he got from me was that Justin was in surgery 'cause Daddy jumped on him. He was the one who told me not to tell Daddy that bullshit in the first place. He did wonder out loud where we would go. I didn't even know other than the hell out of Georgia.

"Chicago? My birth family there."

"Your birth family?"

I thought I knew everything about the man, I was second-guessing the whole time I was packing up the bathroom. When we met he said his father was named John so he went by Calvin.

"Naw, my lady, I didn't say the man's *last* name was 'Mitchell'. His name *is* John Calvin though."

"Oh, ok. I didn't know that."

"You know my moms though. She the only family that count for real. That's the lady who took me in. After her husband left it was just me and her. I think she did a pretty good job."

"You got any brothers and sisters out there?"

"I don't know what that man was up to Love. I might."

"Damn, for real?"

"Yeah, real talk."

"So what *would* my last name have been if your mother didn't adopt you?"

"Sanders"

"Sanders?"

"Yeah. Would've been John Sanders."

"That's my grandfather's name! That's a coincidence!"

"Is it? Your last name was Hamilton when we got married. You was hooked up before and didn't run that by me or something?"

"NO! Why would I not tell you something like THAT? Daddy took us in after my real dad passed away. We was little, so Tawana's dad, Mitchell Hamilton took care of us too. Me and Justin started going by his last name so we made it legal. My dad's name was Jacob. Jacob Sanders."

"Man…you know what wifely? I got an uncle named Jacob. Uncle Jake. That would be tripped out if we was some kin. That would be some ole reaping-what-you-sow shit."

"That's what my daddy used to say all the time and I didn't know what he was talking about: Be not deceived; God is not mocked: for whatsoever a man soweth, that shall he also reap."

"What that mean?"

"Basically that you will pay for what you did to somebody, like a consequence of your actions."

"I don't know, but this some weird shit."

"I know right? You think we should try to find out? If it's the same person or not? What if your uncle was my DADDY??? That would mean me and you are cousins!!!"

"We need to know. 'Cause we married. We can't be no married couple if we some kin to each other. That's some weird shit. Lemme call my cousin Rick up and ask him about Uncle Jake. Dude know the whole family on that side. All them from Chicago."

"Please call him"

"Aye whas up Rick? What's going with you? Yeah man nothing much. Just stayin' out the way. That's what's up. Aye man, how Uncle Jake doing?"

"Jake? Man Jake cooler than a fan. What's up? You need to holler at him about something?"

"Naw, man. Just trying to see what's going on with all my kin folk. You know how it is, man. I don't know my real family too much."

"Right. I feel you. Jake a good dude, though, man. He don't be hanging out in the streets like that, he married now. Got a couple kids. You just missed a good party. He rented a boat out for his birthday last week."

"Babe! It ain't him. It ain't your pops. Jacob just had a party and all that."

"Oh my God! I was going to DIE if it was him! My dad died when I was a little girl!"

"What was that man? I can't hear you. It's loud as hell in this plant."

"I was talking to my wife. We was sitting up here talking and she thought she knew Uncle Jake. The person she talkin' 'bout died some years back though."

"*Uncle* Jake? My bad, my dude, I ain't hear you say *Uncle*. I thought you was talking about Junior. Yeah Uncle Jacob died over 20 years ago. I thought you meant his son – we just call him 'Junior' or Jake."

"I didn't know he had kids, man,"

"That's why we need to get together sometimes cuzzo. You gotta get to know your folks, man. Uncle Jacob had 3 kids if I ain't mistaken. He had lil' Jake then Jacobi and Justin with his wife in Georgia. We ain't never met them before though."

The End

Weep What You Sow

Made in the USA
Middletown, DE
30 January 2022

59292508R00091